LAND
of NOD

Peggy C. Gardner

ISBN: 978-1-941142-70-7

For my sister, Patsy, who in Amy Lowell's words, encouraged "a thousand tight-rope tricks" and never tired of watching me "somersault all day."

CHAPTER 1

February 28, 2013
Somewhere in Northern Idaho

The coarse strands of inky hair that he had carefully oiled into submission lopped across his forehead like an unruly tuft on a warthog. The thick-necked man carried his fifty years gingerly, as though a phantom belly waited to attach itself. A smile that never reached his eyes lifted his plump reddish lips as he took in the prized female cargo in his just-purchased Chrysler.

The china blue eyes of his new wife were fixed on the treacherous gravel road ahead and wide open, with nothing of much interest behind them. He patted her leg, pleased that this widow's curves were all in the right places, like warm summer peaches on a low-hanging branch.

The proof of her fertility, the splendid plunder of his two-week expedition to Portland, slept in the back seat: a seven-year-old baby doll named Lorena whose peevish nature could be easily corrected and fifteen-year-old Jenny with a glorious mop of chestnut hair, a pouting mouth that could be put to good use, and odd topaz eyes that seemed to see right through him.

For now, all three females were his for the guiding and, eventually, the taking. One, legally, by a civil service marriage in Oregon—and the daughters who would be sealed to him, along with their mother, tomorrow by Ordinance in the Zion Chapel.

If Elder Bonner had any notion that the teenage girl might be handed over as a bride for his fat son, he would make it clear that his daddy had left him almost a quarter of the land in the Ward; the Darken name was still on the deed.

An Elder held sway over an Apostle like him. But with his property, his two wives—unhappily barren— and this new fertile wife with healthy daughters, a summons should be forthcoming for membership in the Quorum that would carry Elder status.

As an Elder, he could act without question as long as the sacraments were kept. Brigham Young had fifty-five wives, sixteen of them widows. He trailed his fingers up his wife's leg, glancing back first to be sure the girls were sleeping. This pretty woman would keep him entertained until that cat-eyed beauty in the back seat had a little more flesh on her—and a little less sass coming out of her mouth.

Jenny would never make it to the Final Tier of Obedience as a preferred wife. She prickled like a cactus from the minute he was announced as her new daddy. She had too many questions—sharp, analytical, as though she already knew the answers. Too much education leached the usefulness out of girls. He'd assign her to a heavy work detail for a year. After that, breaking her to his will would be a piece of cake.

"Whoops. Almost forgot." He shot a sly glance over at his new wife and thumbed a number on his cell phone. "Maylene. Just remembered. We need one of your nice cakes up at the Retreat. We'll be at the compound in an hour."

Portland, Oregon
Earlier that morning

When I pushed off the lumpy comforter with those fat-lipped sock monkeys ogling me, I knew that my fifteenth birthday today could not be worse than my last. A purplish sky outside hung low over the city. An invisible emanation of something threatening—such as my mother's odd behavior all week—dampened any hopes for a happy day.

Last February 28th, I commemorated my birthday at Portland's Mt. Calvary Cemetery, dry-eyed with anger as wet clumps of snow pelted a 12 by 12-makeshift tent above James Hatchet's coffin.

Why couldn't my father, who loved Euclid's geometry as much as I did, keep his truck going from one point to the other and back? From Portland to Bend and back without a zigzag into the McKenzie River?

My mother's mascara zigzagged down her cheeks as I tried not to look at the bilious fake grass below my father's coffin. She had just startled me by announcing: "Your father's brother Hal should have been here." Having an uncle was news to me.

Unwelcome news. The wrong brother was balanced above a grave. Each strap was equidistant from the next. Being a stickler for exact spatial positioning, I checked out the corners of the wind-whipped tent. Euclid was wrong. It is not true that all right angles are equal to one another. It is not true that the whole is greater than the part.

That day, the best part of our family dropped into a grave—and there was no way to make us whole again. So, I'm ashamed to say, I pinched my seven-year-old sister Lorena until she stopped crying and screeched at me in front of the pitifully few mourners. Anger is a better public defense than tears.

Clara, my stunning mother, with her Shirley Temple dimples and golden sausage curls, didn't have heart for anger, so she let the bank take the mortgage, had a yard sale, and moved us to a one-bedroom apartment in the sleazy part of Portland.

A woman who had only skills for loving her husband and daughters ended up working double shifts, shelving at the Price-and-Carry where out-of-date food was hers for the taking.

Careful not to wake Lorena so early this morning, I inched away from the bed where her asthmatic breathing quickened the sock monkeys so that they seemed to hover above her head like the evil winged primates in the *Wizard of Oz.*

I sized up Jenny Hatchet in the streaky mirror on our bedroom door. She was a year older but no different from the day before, with a mass of unruly hair longing to work itself into curls if allowed, and a body toned from daily runs.

The first half of Jenny's sophomore year in a new school went just as she had expected: first place in the high school 10K Challenge; algebra mastered; breezing into pre-calc, and, no one she could call a best friend. She'd left them on the other side of Portland.

She frowned at the image of a girl who wished she could quit trying to excel so that she could be ordinary; she might even be popular. If only she didn't feel compelled to pass all those thrashing legs ahead of her, if only she didn't absolutely love working with numbers, if only . . . . Her yellowish-green cat's eyes would be disturbing if they were not exactly like her father's.

My annoying habit of critiquing myself in third person gave me a reassuring distance, kept the nagging "me" at bay.

As for *me*, I wasn't expecting much for my birthday—just a freshly baked Price and Carry cake with glue-like frosting and sugar roses. Mother should be arriving from her night shift at any moment with my birthday surprise.

I had overhauled and oiled the rusty lock so that her key could turn the bolt easily while she balanced a cake. The front door swung wide. A murky shadow behind my mother blocked the light.

In the most mellifluous voice she could fabricate, she announced: "Girls, meet your new father—Gomer Obadiah Darken."

GOD slithered into the room, oozing his way over to Lorena who stood in the bedroom door with her hands stuffed into her mouth; then, he whipped around and clamped on to me with a hug that would shame a python. Unlike boa constrictors, pythons don't crush their victims; they simply squeeze them slowly until they suffocate.

When Gomer Obadiah Darken detached his hands from an artful fondle of my rigid neck, he unfolded into a six-foot man with a thatch of black hair sticking straight up like a shoeshine brush. Small wisps of the same black hair tickled the edge of each nostril.

His wide, pasted-on smile revealed an excess of teeth, the bottom row all crammed together and jagged like a piranha. He moved with a certain flair, casually shedding a tan cashmere coat that rippled like silk, and lifted a stiffening Lorena onto his knees as he settled onto the only good chair.

"Clara, dear heart, you forgot and left Jenny's birthday present in the hall. Can you fetch it while I get acquainted with your daughters—*our daughters*." It wasn't a question. He managed to reprimand my mother and lay claim to Lorena and me in the same breath—a maneuvering man from the get-go. I circled behind the sofa and narrowed my eyes.

They widened with a jolt when my mother rolled in a hot pink suitcase covered with Barbie's profile—as though the plastic doll had procreated like a rabbit but turned aside so that she wouldn't have to observe her warren.

"It's for our trip today. You girls will simply love our new home. Mr. Darken—you'll soon want to call him daddy—has a big acreage in Northern Idaho where he lives with friends and relatives. Sort of a protected compound he says with creeks pure as spring water running through it and all kinds of animals for you girls to tend."

Lorena struggled to get off Mr. Darken's lap, but her eyes had taken on a transfixed stare, the kind of expression she gets when watching reruns of *Lassie*.

"Animals?" Because of her asthma, we couldn't have a pet.

"Cows, goats, horses, chickens, dogs and cats. You name it. We've got it. Your mama told me about your asthma. Fresh, country air will cure you in a flash. City living wears out the lungs. You can't get out of this smog too soon. Get yourselves packed."

I watched Humbert Humbert tracing the tips of his fingers along the nape of Lorena's neck, toying with the damp curls, extending his palms across her thin shoulders, owning her before he even knew her. No stranger owned my family or me.

I could feel blood swelling the capillaries in my eyeballs; they must have been red as a vampire's when I spoke. Not to him. To my mother. "We live in Portland. We like it here. We like our school. We like our apartment. We like our neighborhood." My voice was beginning to sound like one of those old wax records with a bad scratch, but I recovered and shouted: "We're not going anywhere!"

"You will do exactly what your mother tells you to do." Mr. Darken's voice was so quiet I had to strain to hear him—it was a voice that does not broker deals. "This apartment is in a slum. You girls and your mother deserve a better life, in a community of God-fearing people. I had to kick a drunk Indian out of the way just to get inside the lobby of this building." His self-righteous tone raised the hairs on the back of my neck.

"You let him kick Mr. Tomeh? He's harmless. Just sleeps over the vent."

Mother sidled around the sofa, with an uneasy glance toward her new husband, and threw her arms around my neck. "Oh, Jenny, why are you being difficult? You know the insurance didn't cover part-time drivers. Funeral expenses were . . . we've been living hand to mouth for . . ." her voice trailed off; her pale blue eyes appeared almost opaque, as though looking out of them tired her.

She stepped away from me with a sense of purpose that unnerved me. "I thought this would be a wonderful birthday surprise. We're going to have a nice home. Gather up the things you need. We won't be coming back here. Mr. Darken will take care of us, the way your father took care of us."

I didn't think so. I grabbed the Barbie roller bag and swept past Mr. Darken with all the hauteur I could muster, considering my outgrown Hello Kitty pajamas and matted hair.

I didn't need clothes where we were going. We wouldn't be staying there for long. Mother would see the error of her ways. She and my father had been high school sweethearts.

"Death ends a life—not a relationship." Mother found that in a book of quotations and had it carved on a stone that was too large for our small bank account. That, alone, must mean that Mr. Darken was only a passing fancy, a glitch in her judgment. I would go along for the ride but only as a reluctant passenger.

The Barbie bag bulged in every direction. The first order of business was to pack all the half-repaired clocks that Daddy and I had collected from flea markets; the second was to put in all my tools for electrical repair work.

I wired lamps, replaced fuses, and did odd electrical jobs for the apartment manager to help cover our rent— Daddy was an electrician before he took up truck driving for better pay. For as long as I could remember, I had been his apprentice.

I might need 8-gauge, 10-gauge, 14-gauge and 18-gauge wire no matter what kind of appliances were in Mr. Darken's house. Surely he would have an Internet connection. We couldn't afford connectivity in the apartment, so I often trotted down to the golden arches after school with my MacBook. Padded with a towel, my Mac tested Barbie's zipper to the breaking point.

Lorena hummed Taylor Swift's "We Are Never Ever Getting Back Together" as she made obsessively neat piles of t-shirts, jeans, underwear, and put toiletries in a small plastic bag. She eased the pile into her duffle bag, stopped humming, and swept her collection of plastic horses into the bag. "Just in case he doesn't really have any horses." She picked up where she left off with Taylor, droning through sealed lips as though she knew she would annoy someone more than me.

I crammed a toothbrush, a hairbrush, pajamas and spare underwear into the exterior pocket of the bag. The cheap stitching along the side was already fraying. I shoved my Nintendo with Mario and Grand Theft Auto Chinatown into the pocket of my jacket. If Mr. Darken didn't have the Internet, I could still help Huang Lee get the sword from the Angels of Death and the Korean Mob.

Maybe my little sister would stay quiet in the car by helping Mario leap the evil mushrooms. If she didn't stop humming soon, I would be tempted to disembowel the frog radio she was struggling to push into her duffle.

Groping under the mattress into a hole I'd made, I pulled out the $80 I got a week ago from an antique store just off Taylor for a mantel clock that my father had picked up for next to nothing. It was the last clock we worked on together—such a beautiful thing inside with all those wheels and gears and perfectly balanced weights.

"People have been keeping time with obelisks and hourglasses and flowing water for eons, but mechanical clocks have been around for less than a thousand years—much more beautiful inside than outside, don't you think, Jenny?" Daddy had ruffled my hair and headed off for that fatal drive.

Last week, the man in the antique store had eyed me suspiciously as I spun out a story about my grandmother. She died long before I was born, so I didn't think that she'd mind getting one of those drug-resistant TB strains.

"Mycobacteria. She needs the money. I disinfected the clock, so it's perfectly safe." He shoved a small wad of cash at me as I flashed my best gimlet-eyed stare. We both knew he'd quadruple the price. My tears weren't for my infected grandmother; they were for the last clock my father would ever repair.

I shoved the bills into my sock the moment Lorena turned to hear muffled voices coming through the cheap paneling on the walls. The cash might be enough for bus tickets back to Portland.

Mother eased the bedroom door open, moved over beside us and planted a soft, sad kiss on the top of Lorena's head and a lingering one on my right cheek. Mother usually wasn't so demonstrative. Then, she stepped around the end of the bed and struggled to slide the closet door open as it skidded off track as usual.

As I moved over to scoot it back into place, she pulled out a large suitcase hidden at the back. "Don't bother with that closet door. I'm already packed. I just need to get my make-up bag. Mr. Darken is waiting outside in his Chrysler—the big black one just down the street. I helped him pick it out yesterday." Her face flushed as though she had been caught with her hand in the till.

I shot my Judas-faced mother one of my hard-assed looks. She had already packed her bag. That meant Mr. Darken was not a birthday surprise. Judas Iscariot betrayed Jesus with a kiss and cash. I guess a Chrysler cost a lot more than thirty pieces of silver.

CHAPTER 2

The Chrysler's plump leather seats were squashy past imagining. Lorena dozed off instantly as I fought sleep. I watched Mother's newly ringed hand moving in an undulating motion like one of those cheap plastic Chinatown fans across Mr. Darken's shoulders as he hunched over the steering wheel and muttered about Portland traffic.

"We've got to go back! Turn around, Gomer."

Relief flooded me like a spring rain. Mother had come to her senses.

"I forgot my makeup case. All the things I need are in it." The wavering words "I need" struck me as very close to the heart of things. Moisturizers, bottles of pale ivory foundation, and tubes of lipstick might reverse a car. Two anxious daughters in the backseat wouldn't.

"Not necessary, my sweet girl. Replaceable. We need to get home before dark. The commuter traffic this morning has delayed us. Besides, you don't need anything on that pretty face."

Before he made it to the 84 exit, Portland's skyline began to disappear in the morning haze, slowly receding, the way our lives would vanish when we got to some-where in the boonies of Idaho.

The year since my father's death had tested us in ways we couldn't imagine, and all of us—my sister, my mother, and me—had failed to be as brave as he would have expected us to be.

Lorena began wetting the bed. Instead of helping her drag the sheets to soak in the claw-footed tub, I whipped off the sheets when the dampness oozed into my sleep and yelled at my sister—that wheezy, drip-nose, china-doll facsimile of my mother, the child that I loved better than anyone on this planet.

As for my mother, she was born to tap dance to "The Good Ship Lollipop" without noticing that it was a Douglas DC-2. The only child of elderly parents, my cherished mother simply changed her residence when she married my doting father. He earned; she spent. As a journeyman electrician, he made good wages. With a wife who believed that plastic cards offered endless credit, my father had to balance their bank account by climbing into a semi as a part-time driver.

When he skidded into the McKenzie River, Mother's world went off balance. She had no market-able skills. She would have graced a make-up counter beautifully, but she couldn't figure out how to work the register.

After my father died, the first person to comfort her was the funeral home director. Assuring my mother that a "hand-rubbed teak" casket, a cement vault, and an onyx headstone that could rival a pagan king's would be the "only way to remember her husband as he deserved," the funeral director slithered away with my father's life insurance policy and the balance of his bank account.

Three months later, we were sharing a bedroom in an apartment where the carpet smelled of cat piss and the manager was desperate enough to let a fourteen-year-old rewire worn-out cook tops and ovens as long as she kept her mouth shut.

GOLDEN ARCHES REACHED heavenward off to the east as Mr. Darken pushed the Chrysler just over the speed limit.

"I'm hungry. I want some McNuggets. There! There! Turn around, Mr. Darken. You missed the access road." Lorena's high, peevish voice traveled on a curving trajectory into the front seat.

"We don't need gas yet. We stop when we do. It's five more hours to Bonner's Ferry, then another hour on dirt roads. Driving in the dark is hazardous. You girls should know that, considering what happened to your father."

The sharp intake of Mother's breath made a more explosive sound than the thump of my shoe against the driver's seat. "Gomer, the girls didn't have breakfast. They must be starving." Her voice had assumed a wheedling tone that only irritated me. Mr. Darken's reference to my father infuriated me. I drew back my leg for another whack at the back of his seat when Mother flashed me a warning glance.

"I need a bathroom break, my dear. I'm sure everyone would welcome a stretch and a snack." She caressed the back of a neck that sprouted chimpanzee-like hair.

He whipped the Chrysler over to an off-ramp and pulled up next to a Quik-Rest gas pump. "Bathrooms inside. Hurry back to the car. I can't wait to get my little family home." He beamed over at our mother as though Santa had just left him the biggest package under the tree. "I'll get things for lunch. Some treats."

The caustic odor of disinfectant did nothing to mask the chipped, filthy linoleum and empty toilet paper rolls. I pushed Lorena's hands under near-boiling water and used my foot to shove the door handle.

The sacks in Mr. Darken's hands looked promising. They weren't. We were on the 84 again and moving fast with the mid-day traffic while Lorena sent up a new round of complaints as Mother pulled out of one sack: a loaf of white bread, a package of bologna, a sack of peeled baby carrots that had taken on the white glaze of age, and four paper cups that Mr. Darken had swiped from the self-serve coffee stand.

The second sack held a gallon of water marked "distilled" and a sack of cookies that were meant to resemble zoo animals with a nasty, pinkish glaze on them.

I rolled small pills of white bread all the way to the Idaho state line and shoved them under Mr. Darken's seat. Rotten bologna would stink up the car better, but Mother knew not to pass it back to us. Lorena and I wouldn't touch the stuff. Made of cow spleens and bull peckers. That's what some kids at school told me, and I made sure that Lorena never developed a taste for it.

I KNEW BETTER than to comment with GOD behind the wheel, but Lorena spouted off like Mt. Etna before I could wrestle her into silence. "I said I wanted McNuggets. Or a coke. Or just a sack of chips. I'm not particular. Anyone can tell you that. We take turns choosing." Her thin voice had lost its injured tone and settled for the hopefulness of fair play.

"Do you know what 'Theodemocracy' means, Lorena?" Mr. Darken's question sounded rhetorical, but Lorena didn't take the bait.

"Yes. George Washington and Abraham Lincoln and everyone who dumped tea did it to free the slaves and fight the British." Lorena's assured response to Mr. Darken's question pretty much covered the waterfront as far as I was concerned. I gazed out at passing cars so I wouldn't have to meet his eyes in the rearview mirror.

"I take it that your school didn't spend much time on American history. No matter. You'll be in a private school where we live. Theodemocracy has to do with God and his people ruling in righteousness. You'll soon learn that word."

I intercepted the cloud nine smile Mother was sending in Mr. Darken's direction. I knew that she had heard the words "private school" and was busily conjuring up images of tidy uniforms and well-off parents who could afford the best for their children.

"God and his people ruling in righteousness" sent a chill down my spine. I had the feeling that Mr. Darken and the First Amendment weren't exactly on speaking terms.

Lorena, bored by the topic, drooled pink animal cookie dye, as she slept open-mouthed. I watched wide-eyed as Northern Idaho unfolded its mountains and lakes and plowed winter fields like a video designed for the tourist trade. Portland had a special beauty, but this magnificent scenery seemed to be sweeping me into a wilderness empty past imagining.

THE CAR SLOWING down woke me from a deep and troubled sleep. The driver's window slid silently open, and Mr. Darken pushed in numbers on a keypad as a huge, slatted, metal gate rolled back. I watched him hit "6" with a cupped hand four times.

My window would only roll partway down, but I stuck my head out and tried to see through the heavy darkness surrounding the car. The lights flashed on a packed gravel road ahead. To the right, I could see a semicircle of lights in windows of one and two-story structures as well as clusters of lights in the distance.

A barn loomed behind big corrals to the left; small spotlights splayed weak beams of light on smaller buildings. A couple of men waved in our direction and headed back inside the barn.

Mr. Darken said: "Late snow; early calves. Had to move the heifers down. That's Elder Bonner over there by the corral. You'll meet him tomorrow, Clara. He'll be officiating at our celestial marriage."

That shook me awake faster than an off-key bugle. Mother had told us that GOD was her husband. That's what she said when she brought him to our apartment this morning. I fidgeted with undisguised pleasure. We could get out of this mess. Be on our way. Hello Portland.

In the most controlled voice I could muster that sounded rougher than the gravel road beneath us, I said: "Then, you're not married. You're just thinking about it."

Mr. Darken snorted with something that might have passed for laughter if joy could come from a dark place. "Civil ceremony, Jenny. Under Oregon law. Your mother wanted it that way, so I obliged. We're legal all right. But, not in our religion." He chucked Mother under the chin with what I observed to be a bit too forceful for a newlywed.

Right after my father died, Mother gave in to her guilt on Sunday mornings and would drag us to the nearest Baptist or Methodist or Christian church. She said she chose a Catholic cemetery for my father because it was "more permanent."

When she said that, I had visions of large, earth-moving equipment scooping up graves and splintered coffins and bone fragments, transplanting them piece-meal to higher ground—the way they do when a dam is built to flood a deserted town.

Lately, we had been sleeping in on Sunday mornings and talking the rest of the day about how we should have gone to church. Mother could procrastinate like a champion. She sat with zipped lips now.

"What religion?" The words squeaked past my lips as though someone else had uttered them.

"The only one, sweet Jenny. Our own priestly line through David. You're sitting in the car with one right now though I can't perform the sealing with my own wife. I'm an Apostle, soon to be an Elder. Some people call us by an old name, The Saints."

I knew that GOD wasn't referring to a New Orleans football team.

He touched the electric seat adjustment and slid back, pinning my legs against the seat. "Our official name is the Church of the Protectors of Restoration Christianity—CPRC. Our ward here is one of several in this state and others. The ordinance will take place tomorrow. Your mother and I will be sealed for eternity—in this world and the next."

A dreadful sense of apprehension made me break out in a heavy sweat—as though I had run twice my daily 10K and couldn't stop. If such a thing as another world existed, my father would be looking for his beloved wife and this Joseph Smith look-alike would have her sealed up like an Egyptian mummy in his own pyramid.

"There's the Retreat—our temporary home for a few days until we sort things out." Mr. Darken flashed the lights on bright. He need not have bothered. Giant floodlights spread a blast of light for fifty yards in every direction. A WWII prisoner of war camp had less security.

CHAPTER 3

A Swiss chalet on steroids popped out of the side of a mountain like a great pustule, oozing window boxes filled with artificial flowers, faded and tattered from the harsh winter.

The trunk of the car popped open. "Get your bags and get out of this night air. It's still winter in this part of the world. You might need help with yours, Jenny. I think you put bricks in it." His guffaw was the only sound in the night.

I brushed past him, swung the Barbie bag out and carried it without the aid of that flimsy pull and wheels that now straddled sideways with fatigue.

Lorena grabbed her duffle and put a thumb in her mouth. Wetting the bed was the least of her problems. She was moving back into some infantile state. I pulled her close to me and clomped up the stairs to our temporary home.

A cast-iron stove sent cascades of heat waves partway through the room. The rich aroma of some kind of hot dish drew us near a table that had been covered and set for four with real cloth napkins.

Mr. Darken grabbed a dishtowel and lifted the lid. "My . . . uh . . . the women have done themselves proud. Venison stew and fresh baked bread." He pointed to a mound of whole wheat bread that didn't resemble any of the preservative-laden loaves at Price and Carry.

I tried to control a faint shudder. Venison. I wasn't eating Bambi. Just before I geared up to offer my lecture on the evils of hunting wild animals, Mother let out a squeal. "Look at that, Jenny. Angel food cake with seven minute frosting! I haven't seen one of those since my own mother baked one for me every birthday."

I had never seen one. It stood at least eight inches tall and gleamed with frosting the color of snow.

"I'll show you the honeymoon suite before we eat, Clara." There was something particularly inhospitable about his voice at the moment, confirmed by his next statement.

"Jenny, the women who fixed us this nice meal and your birthday cake, Maylene and Marybeth—you'll get to know them better soon—hung some dresses in your closet for you and Lorena to wear to the ceremony tomorrow. My girls will all look like pretty flowers."

I wanted to snarl. *I'll be the foxglove—digitalis, Dead Man's Bells, Witches' Gloves.* It was the "my girls" that pissed me off worse than his reference to us as flowers.

"You share the bedroom down the hall." He jutted a fat thumb down the bleak hall, away from the wood-burning stove.

Only the Spartans could have decorated a room more austerely. Two small cots were stacked on top of each other. An ugly veneered dresser that looked as if it had made the rounds of several flea markets stood against the only wall with a window.

Lorena eased over to the closet and opened the door. She had spells of being fond of dresses, especially if they had skirts of tulle and velvet tops. These didn't. I couldn't imagine where anyone could find fabric with designs from the fifties, big green and blue flower vases dripping with daisies. Where did they find patterns with dropped waists and capped sleeves? These were hand-made dresses but not from an upscale designer house.

I eased the door closed on the horrors. Lorena had resumed sucking her thumb with a vengeance. "We can wear our jeans. Let's go eat."

Mother and Mr. Darken were sitting silently, but his fingers drummed impatiently against the table. His bowl was full to the brim. "Promptness at meals is an expecta-tion. You'd do well to remember that."

Mother lifted the top from the venison stew. I had to admit that the odor was tantalizing, but I frowned until she fished around for onions, carrots, and potatoes with just a smidgen of Bambi juice.

When Mother scooped several pieces of meat into Lorena's bowl, my mouth flew open and shifted to half-mast the minute I saw Mother's plaintive expres-sion. The pale child with stains from animal cookies on her shirt needed protein. I'd just have to pretend that it wasn't something that frolicked with the antelope.

Before any of us could grab a spoon, Mr. Darken folded his hands into a fleshy tent, closed his hooded eyes, and prayed. He prayed for the "union." I don't think he meant the U. S. of A. He prayed for the lost souls of unguided children. He prayed for the bounteous meal. And he prayed that we would be "sealed" in happiness for eternity.

I had never put too much effort into thinking about eternity. If it existed, I was sure that everything in it would line up perfectly, that all the angles would be absolutely equidistant, and that the most interesting people who had ever lived would sit around scented fountains and talk to me. Euclid and John Paul Jones and Cleopatra if she could get out of her mummy garb. Of course, my father would be there. And Mother and Lorena. But not for a very long time.

I looked at the end of the table where Mr. Darken was wolfing down a second bowl of stew without so much as of a swipe of that nice cloth napkin to degrease his chin. I would rather be locked up with thermal radiation than with Mr. Darken for eternity. Every time I looked at him, I could feel my eyes sloughing off a layer of tissue.

CHAPTER 4

The night was colder than cold and the bed harder than any mattress had a right to be. I piled my blanket on top of a shivering Lorena and slept in my clothes.

A thin sliver of light streaming through the window above the dresser woke me from an uneasy sleep. I boosted myself up and saw Douglas fir and Lodgepole pine encircling the periphery of the property like a stockade. Just through an open patch in the evergreens, I could see a faint line that might be a path or a deer trail.

I needed to run, at least for thirty minutes, more if I could fit it in. A day of riding in the car, topped off with cake last night that was actually the best I'd ever tasted, made me sluggish.

Pulling on my hoodie with Bob Marley's face on it, I sped down the hall and out the door. A blast of sleet-teased wind hit my face. Mr. Darken was right about one thing—the pine-scented air was wonderful. I sprinted across the frost-packed yard and headed down a path between the trees.

In the distance I could see the larger compound with its hog-wire fencing and eight-inch diameter wooden corner posts. From this distance, I could see insulators on the posts. The fence was electrified. A deer might clear it or a rabbit go through it, but nothing else could get in or out.

A group of small sheds lined the trail just ahead. If I skirted them, I could stay out of sight on the near side of the trees, but get close enough to the fence to see how many houses and buildings were in the compound.

A loud noise, like metal clashing, erupted. I whirled around the corner of the far shed and missed seeing the fat leg in a stiff boot that sent me crashing onto my back. The face that looked down at me faintly resembled Donnie Osmond, except the perfect teeth had been replaced by badly stained, irregular incisors. Donnie had gained a few pounds and had a very heavy foot that was planted just on top of my solar plexus.

There was nothing musical about the voice: "What's a girl doing running around our property in pants?"

I couldn't decide on the answer. Was running or wearing pants the greater offense?

"Girls don't wear men's clothes here." The foot stayed where it was.

Obviously, running wasn't the offense. But, his foot was. I struggled to move with 200 pounds pushing me into the frozen tundra.

"Let me up, you jerk!" He had lifted his boot just long enough for me to gasp out an insult. The foot moved as his hand latched onto my arm, pulled me upright, and shook me until I could feel my bones rattling.

"Enoch Bonner, if Mr. Darken catches you abusing his new stepdaughter, there won't be enough hide left on your backside to keep you warm." The voice was low but clear as a bell.

The fingers popped from around my arm as quickly as though they had grabbed onto a hot poker. "How was I to know this was her? I seen someone running like something was chasing them. Then slowing down to nose around. That's when I tripped her—before I seen it was a girl. In pants. Pa wouldn't like that and he says what's what around here."

The fat facsimile of Donnie had moved back, but he was winding himself up like an eight-day clock. "You don't have no say-so here Josh Barnes. You don't have a pa, and your ma never got claimed. You don't have no voice."

"I don't need one. I have these." The boy who was positioning himself as an out-fighter, distancing himself carefully to control the first punch, looked more like Jude Law than Jude Law, same pale blue eyes, blonder hair, and a half-cocked grin that was clearly irritating Enoch Bonner more than his words.

"Bring it on, or do you just bully helpless girls?"

Enoch slouched back a couple of steps. He had fifty pounds on this boy named Josh, but I had no doubt who would win this match. Faint grunting sounds could be heard, but neither one had struck a blow.

The "helpless girls" comment riled me. That freak of nature had caught me off guard. I could outrun him any day of the week, but I was scrunched up like a rag doll that had been carelessly dropped along the path with Enoch's big, hobnailed boot dangerously near.

The giant who stepped from between the two sheds might have been the Hunchback of Notre Dame until he swung his hump free and dropped it between the two boys. A line of golden, shelled corn spilled from the gunnysack. "Either one of you step across that line, and you'll reckon with me. What's going on here, Enoch?"

The man in charge clearly favored Enoch—right down to the thatch of dark hair, squared-off jaw, and the right to tell his side first.

"I saw someone running across the field and into the woods in a suspicious manner, Pa. I thought someone might be after them. So, I waited by the shed there. I think she tripped."

"Yeah. Over your boot that ended up on her stomach as she lay helpless on the ground." Josh had lowered his fists, but stood glaring at both the man and Enoch.

"You'll have a chance to have your say, Josh. Keep a civil tongue in your mouth while I hear my boy out."

"You can hear me out, Mr. Bonner. I was out for an innocent morning run when your son tripped and stomped me." Two small lies. I *had* been scouting out the compound, and Enoch had weighed me down with his boot, not really stomped. I wanted Josh Barnes to know that I could manage my own defense with a little pizzazz around the edges.

"Both you boys scoop up that corn! Get the sows fed before they bust out." He waved a clenched fist toward one of the sheds.

The grunting sounds hadn't come from two angry boys but a pen of fat hogs, snorting, butting each other with slimy snouts, and wallowing in a foot of thick mud. Their greedy eyes were frightful, nothing like Charlotte's pink friend, Wilbur. Lorena would be in for a shock.

The hand that pulled me up was thick with calluses but gentle as it brushed fir needles off my back. "Let's get you up to the Retreat. Your folks will be worried about you." He moved decisively ahead of me on the path as though "ladies first" never entered his head.

THE SOUND OF a child crying uncontrollably stopped us at the edge of the porch of a chalet that looked shabbier in the light of day, the fake geraniums in the window boxes faded to a sickly color of rust. Mr. Bonner hesitated, and then loped off back toward the compound.

"I'm not wearing that goofy flowered dress. And I don't want *him* telling me I'll learn to like it. I won't. I hate ugly clothes." Lorena's shrill voice peaked with fury and wound down like a prisoner finally stepping up to the gallows.

The rows of pink taffeta cascading down from a modest neckline to her ankles suggested that my mother was bound for her first prom—or her wedding as a less than virginal bride. Her face was ashen, but I noted a faint blue line of eye shadow on her upper lids. GOD had not found the hidden stash of makeup in her purse.

"Can you deal with your sister, Jenny? She's been acting out all morning—ever since she woke up and couldn't find you. The Sealing Ceremony is scheduled in an hour. Mr. Darken says his religion requires females to wear dresses. This isn't what I . . . what he . . . what I had in mind but he says . . ." The thought she had been pursuing drifted off.

The grayish-blue emptiness in my mother's eyes might have spurred me to seize the moment and try to convince her that this Idaho trip had been a bad mistake, one that could be remedied. With GOD standing in the doorway in a stiff black suit, this was not the moment.

"Could you get her to dress, Jenny? She'll listen to you. The Sealing Ceremony is an important ritual for Gomer." I was close enough to Mother to see a faint sprinkling of freckles under a glaze of perspiration. Mother's over-priced vanishing creams were gone. She was vanishing without them.

I looked up into her vacuous eyes; her half-smile didn't reach her eyes, as though she'd come to terms with her bad decision and would spend the rest of her life getting over it.

Ten minutes later, a pouting Lorena in a ghastly lavender concoction of ruffles that hung to her ankles, emerged from our bedroom, one hand in mine, the other in her mouth.

To describe my dress would be an affront to fash-
ionistas from New York to the Sudan. More cannot be
said than ankle-high Converse tennis shoes below a
field of orange and yellow poppies set off by a peplum
would have stunned Carrie Bradshaw into silence.

I placed my hand on the back of Lorena's spine and
whispered. "Stand up straight. Just pretend we're part of
a circus. Lions not monkeys."

CHAPTER 5

Twin odors of camphor and mothballs fought with a single bouquet of aging mums and won as we stepped into the entryway to the Chapel of Zion. A sea of drab wool coats made a post World War II fashion statement about sturdy fabric.

Elder Bonner at the podium nodded to a wizened woman with a knot of gray hair who bent over the keyboard of an upright piano. Mr. Darken signaled us to pause at the back of the aisle like stiff soldiers waiting for martial strains.

They came with amazing clarity and volume. A voice as lush as Adele's belted out: "The morning breaks; the shadows flee." I stood there amazed until the last words hit my solar plexus as hard as Enoch's boot. ". . . bringing ransomed children home."

I tugged on Mr. Darken's arm and put my mouth against his ear. It was as close as I ever planned to come to that hair-sprigged cavity. "Lorena and I are here to watch. If you try to make us part of this sealing thing, I'll scream this place down. I'll use words your congregation has never heard. Against you."

He pointed toward an odd, three-legged stool in the corner of one alcove. "The cucking stool. We still use it here for disobedient women and quarrelsome children. Take your sister and sit on the front pew with your mouth shut. I'll deal with you later."

On the second row of pews from the front, Enoch Bonner sat grinning as though he could hear every word. A string of younger Bonners with the same squared-off jaws and big, brown bovine eyes filled two pews behind him. The same witless expression graced each of their faces. A single pew behind them held an assortment of women—their frozen faces reflected nothing more than endurance.

I scanned the pews. Josh Barnes was nowhere to be seen. Sitting alone on the back pew was a woman with gray-blond strands of hair plaited into a tight wad on her thin neck. Her eyes were the same pale blue as those of Josh. She glanced at me without smiling, lifted her eyes heavenward like some kind of Delphic oracle, and seemed to be waiting for a sign that was reluctant to appear.

The acorn didn't fall far from the tree. Elder Bonner wound himself up like a patriarch of old, sprinkling Bible verses faster than commas. If I heard the word "covenant" once, I heard it a dozen times. Then, with his ham hands on my mother's head, he pronounced that: "truth and good are joined in this covenant of marriage which constitutes heaven itself."

That did it for me. Mother might be sealed. I was sealed off forever from this hokum that felt like something out of the *Bride of Frankenstein*. My Elsa Lanchester mother with her anxious eyes didn't scream in horror. Mr. Darken didn't shout with understanding: "She hate me!"

He simply planted a big, wet kiss on her pale cheek, turned to the pews and lifted her hand with a thin gold band in a kind of salute to the congregation. She no longer wore the two-carat diamond he'd bought her. Too ostentatious, he had told her. Not fitting to wear here.

Members of the Church of the Protectors of Restoration Christianity lined up just off the vestry outside the Community Room. None of the faces looked very welcoming. If lechery could be bottled, all of the males over the age of sixteen must have drunk from it. Even without makeup, my mother radiated a kind of sensual liveliness in comparison to the drab women standing in line.

I was reminded of those World War II films in which lines of dispossessed Jews stood waiting for something more than a stock car to arrive on the train tracks. We were moving along the line, but the women shaking our hands knew what arriving meant.

Tables covered with slabs of home-cured ham, fried chicken, thick soupy chicken and dumplings were only an introduction to something better—the dessert table held wonders I'd never tasted. Brownies packed with pecans, dripping with chocolate frosting, vied with mile-high meringue on lemon pies.

Mr. Darken cornered us as soon as we had filled our plates. He held the arm of a squared-off sturdy woman and steered her toward us. "This nice woman here will drive you girls back to the Retreat. She'll pack your food to take with you and see that you're settled before she leaves. Your mother and I will visit for awhile."

He patted the woman on the back, a little too familiarly for a newly married man, I thought. "You can do that for them, can't you, Maylene." It wasn't a question.

I looked at him blankly. Maylene didn't look at him or me. Mountains of food sat untouched. Girls sat on one side of the room at picnic-style tables; boys sat on the other. Women mingled with women; men with men. Small children dashed around, noisy and free.

"Lorena and I aren't ready to go. We'll just wait here with you and Mother. Lorena might want to get acquainted." I didn't mention myself. I didn't want to know any of these people. I did want another brownie.

"You haven't been Sealed." Mr. Darken spit the last word out as though ridding himself of a bad taste. "After an ordinance, the Community Room is reserved for sealed families only. I let you girls go through the welcoming line as a courtesy to your mother. Your school programs start tomorrow. You'd best get a good night's sleep." He patted Maylene on the back as though touching her was an afterthought.

We sat scrunched three abreast on the front seat of an old pickup as the woman popped the gear into drive. I clutched the basket of our food. Maylene didn't say a word. And then, she did. "Mr. Darken said you liked my cake."

I swung toward her. She was one of the women he mentioned last night—Maylene and Marybeth—the ones who cooked the venison stew and left me an angel food cake for my birthday. "I loved it. I've never had cake like that . . . in my entire life." My voice sounded a bit overwrought. A cake is, after all, just a cake. But, I had a feeling that this woman didn't get many compliments.

Her dark, bushy hair bunched out from her tight-fitting cloche. A scraggly sweater hung off her shoulders as though fashion never crossed her mind. "I'm good at angel food cakes. They sell well at farmers' markets. Town women don't bake much. We make a right smart amount of money selling baked goods and preserves."

Within a few minutes, we were inside, our food on the table, with a fire popping in the wood stove. "Mr. Darken and I." She paused as though there was something important she had to say. "We go back over twenty years. Marybeth almost that long. It's best not to trifle with him, Jenny."

She stopped and flashed me a weak smile, as though my name had sweetened her speech. "You'll get used to our ways. Your mother too. We always do. Food's plentiful here." She turned and walked abruptly out the front door, closing it with a sharp bang.

What did she mean about going "back over twenty years" with Mr. Darken? Did they grow up in this place together? The two of them and Marybeth, whoever she was?

Whatever her warning meant about not trifling with Mr. Darken came as no surprise. He was a vindictive man. Lorena and I got into these tacky dresses just so he could do the big hoopla in front of the church. Then, he kicked us out of the party just as things were looking interesting.

That thing about the cucking stool in that alcove off the vestry. I'd read about those stools. In the old days in the Colonies, people were put on those in public places so they could be pelted with garbage and insulted. Sometimes, they were tied to them and dunked in ponds.

Surely, it was just some kind of antique that they kept in the church—like those Fourteenth Century baptismal fonts in English churches. Or, maybe not. Mr. Darken didn't have a sense of humor from what I'd seen of him.

I watched Lorena tucking into my slice of lemon meringue pie. She could have it. It would keep her occupied while I checked out the "honeymoon suite."

Mother and Mr. Darken would probably be at the dinner for some time. The people in that Community Room looked like the gossipy sort, little cliques forming in every corner by sex and age, my mother in her pink dress looking forlorn, as though she'd been left at the altar.

When I popped on the wall switch in the room at the far end of the hall, I gasped, totally unprepared for the splendor before me. At second glance, I realized it wasn't splendid at all; it was garish.

A king-sized, four-poster bed with a red satin cover occupied the center of the room. Great swaths of red satin—polyester satin, not real satin—swooped down from the top of the bed and bunched into rosettes with pink centers to resemble feverish cabbages.

A white sheepskin rug covered the pine wood floor as though a large animal had molted there.

Mirrored sliding closet doors covered one wall. I could only imagine what might be behind them.

The walls had been painted with a glossy crimson that resembled fresh blood. I opened a big trunk in the corner. It was empty except for pieces of silk-like rope. Probably used to tie up the red satin drapes hanging over the windows.

An old-fashioned boom box sat on a squat table in the corner. I thumbed through the collection of CDs. Guy Lombardo, gospel music by Jim Reeves and Tennessee Ernie Ford, and Bing Crosby. The sound of a car pulling up startled me—almost as much as the taste of whoever had bought the CDs.

I closed the door behind me, skittered down the hall like a frightened mouse, and whispered to Lorena: "I've been right here with you."

"You girls get to your room. You've got a big day ahead of you tomorrow." We had a big evening ahead of us when we got to our room. All of Lorena's jeans had disappeared. The one pair I had been wearing was gone, along with my MacBook and Lorena's frog radio. My old clocks had been carelessly dumped in a corner. But, my tools were carefully folded inside my leather pouch.

I grabbed my hoodie off the floor. My Nintendo was still in the pocket. Whoever had raided our room for jeans must have been put off by Bob's dreadlocks.

I clamped my hand reassuringly on the top of my tennis shoe. The $80 stash was still there. Inside the closet on wooden pegs hung an assortment of floral skirts with elastic waists—one size fits all. Shorter for Lorena. Longer for me. All four of our knees would be well covered.

CHAPTER 6

The fatigue on my mother's face might or might not relate to what went on in that garish red room last night. It didn't bear thinking about. She was standing at the kitchen counter smashing lumps of something that looked very raw. "Sausage. Mr. Darken says he requires sausage and two sunny-side up eggs for breakfast every day. I've never cooked sausage."

Neither had I, but I grabbed a skillet, stuck a match to the gas hissing out of the burner and plopped three clumps of sausage into the pan, being careful to burn the edges and leave the middle pink.

If we were lucky, Mr. Darken would be infected by the parasite trichinosis. In biology class, I read about how the larvae in uncooked pork can turn into worms that migrate to the central nervous system. I eased the oozing mess onto a plate, watched Mr. Darken walking jauntily down the hall, and wondered how long it would be before his heart attack.

"I guess I couldn't expect a beauty like you to have culinary skills." Mr. Darken carved off the burnt sides and beamed across the table at my mother who didn't know whether to smile at a compliment or frown at an insult. GOD was a whiz at backhanded compliments.

"No matter, Clara. We'll only be in the Retreat for our honeymoon week; then we'll move to the main residence. I've been shirking my work, so I'll turn you over to Mrs. Barnes today. She will instruct you in the basic principles of our faith. She used to teach school and do some nursing . . . when she was in the world. She's good at what she does."

"But I thought that the girls and I would . . ."

Mr. Darken interrupted. "A program is in place for girls here based on their age and aptitude. Lorena will be in school with the younger girls. Jenny . . ." he paused, extended the tip of his tongue to dislodge egg yolk crusting in the corner of his mouth. "Jenny, you will be in the Industrial Science Academy with a few of the older girls and some of the women."

That didn't sound like a bad idea. Industrial science could cover anything from wiring circuitry to architecture. I had to tie two big knots in the elastic waist, but finally anchored one of those ghastly floral skirts around me, then, I grabbed Lenora's hand and shot outside to crawl into the backseat of the Chrysler.

I loved being my father's apprentice electrician. Maybe I could show these women a thing or two about avoiding shocks.

Outside a squat cement block building, Mr. Darken handed me over to a beaky nosed, gaunt woman he greeted as "Marybeth."

The women in the reception line after the Sealing Ceremony had all been introduced as "Mizzes," with a long, drawn-out hiss. The woman holding the door ajar looked like an undersized Maylene, with dried, bushy hair like one of those 1950 home permanents gone off.

Odd that he didn't introduce me to either of the women who seemed to be helping him. Probably relatives. Maybe his sisters. I could recommend a good conditioner for the bristly hair they had in common. Or not. Unlike Maylene, this one stared at me with eyes that suggested I might want to mind my Ps and Qs.

"I'll pick her up around five. Tell Maylene to have Lorena ready then."

When Marybeth shoved me through the door, the current hit me—about 10 milliamperes of AC right between the eyes.

A hive of industry buzzed as women in goggles lifted vats of boiling lard off industrial-sized gas burners and moved them to a cooling table. Other women were stirring something in dishpans with wooden spoons. Women in a third group were cutting sheets of plastic to line flat, cardboard boxes.

The Industrial Science Academy was just a step up from a medieval prison. No rotting straw. No chains. No racks. No randy jailers anxious to deflower virgin prisoners. But the thick, steamy air with a faint odor of lye and the scent of old grease made me nauseous and weak in the knees.

Mr. Darken did have a sense of humor after all—gallows humor, dark and cynical. He had unpacked my collection of broken clocks and tools from that tacky Barbie suitcase and invented a learning environment to spark my interest.

"Sion Soap," Marybeth announced. The first words to come out of her mouth hinted of pride. "Boutique (pronounced boo-tick) stores from Seattle down to San Francisco carry our soap. Miz Barnes came up with the name and flavors: Rueful Rosemary, Titillating Thyme, and Serious Sage. Josh does the artwork on a computer and prints the labels right here. We're doing a right smart business."

She handed me goggles with lenses so badly scratched that I waved them away.

"Put them on! Lye is caustic. We had an accident here when some dummy didn't let the lard cool to 95 degrees before adding the lye mixture. A blind girl can't carry her weight around here." Marybeth was obviously in the spirit of OSHA, but her "blind girl" comment seemed a bit insensitive.

"You'll go on the line stirring the lye into cold water. You've got to keep a certain stirring rhythm to prevent lumps. Don't stop until the temperature gets to 95. Then shout 'Ready' and one of the women will take your batch to the cooling line."

She turned with what might have been a sympathetic smile. "A city girl like you better use them gloves." She pointed to a pile of worn cotton gloves. "You'll be working on plain soap, what we use around here."

One of the women stepped aside, shoved a large wooden spoon into my hand and snapped out "Stir" as she moved on down the line. I ignored the gloves. They looked well used.

Once I got the rhythm, I kicked into gear with a kind of panache. "Ow . . . o . . . o . . .o." My shriek decreased in volume as the pain increased in the bubbling crescent across the top of my hand.

"Marybeth! Get over here. This one's managed to get lye on her hand during the first five minutes she's been working." The woman who had initially handed me the wooden spoon grabbed it back and pushed me out of the way as she muttered something about "town girls" and "men not satisfied."

Without a word, Marybeth pulled me toward a table in the corner with half a dozen fold-up chairs around it and shoved me into one. She reached into a plastic cooler and held a clump of ice on my hand.

It hurt even more. "Cool water on burns—not ice. That can make it worse." I had read the *Red Cross Safety Manual* from cover to cover, because Lorena was accident-prone, and Mother panicked at the sight of blood.

"Do it yourself then!" Marybeth seemed to be in a bad mood for someone who hadn't suffered the burn.

I examined the half-inch welt that was shaped like an "S." The pain was subsiding. I hoped the scar stayed there to remind me never to trust anything that Mr. Darken said. Like a tattoo of sorts. A Sion Soap tattoo.

"You're one of the new girls, aren't you? I saw you at the Sealing with Mr. Darken and that pretty woman. Here. Drink this. You'll feel better." A girl with red hair pulled into a kind of snood-like thing sat down beside me and wrapped the fingers on my good hand around a glass of milk.

"Could I have iced tea? I don't like milk."

"You can have iced water. We don't drink tea or coffee or anything that's bad for us. That's in the Word of Wisdom, don't you know?"

I didn't, but I took the glass. "I'll try it." This girl had made the only friendly gesture I'd experienced since coming to this mountain wilderness. Maybe I needed the protein. In the past two days, I'd turned down bologna, venison, and sausage.

"Mrs. Dar . . ." She put her hand over her mouth quickly and looked frightened. "Marybeth asked me to work with you, show you the ropes here. I think we'll start over at the cutting table given your experience."

"Or lack of." I grinned and poked my good hand toward her. "Jenny. Jenny Hatchet."

"Oh. Didn't you take your father's name?"

"Hatchet *is* my father's name. He died a year ago. Some members of my family have longer memories than others."

The lye burn hurt, but my mother's actions during the past few days seared into the very soul of me. No need to dump all that on this girl I'd just met. She was watching me with an odd expression, as though confidences like the one I'd just offered were out of line.

"Abigail Johnson. Abigail with the bad temper to go with this." She pointed to carroty hair peeking through a knitted sack anchored to the back of her head. "I prefer sewing. I'm a whiz at those old treadle Singers. I can't wait to use the electric ones. We even have two of the new computerized ones. Imagine!"

I gulped. Lost for words. I didn't want to imagine hours in front of a sewing machine. That's how women in third-world sweatshops spent their days, with music droning overhead to mask the tedium of fitting the same placket on a different garment hour after hour. Abigail sounded energized at the prospect.

She tucked my hand into the crook of her arm and whispered conspiratorially: "Smile and nod while I show you the cutting area. The nice soap is over there." She waved a hand toward the other side of the room. "This is just laundry and household soap. We all use it. If you act interested, they'll quit watching you. The women who run the soap business are really proud of it. They bring in quite a bit of money."

I perked up. Women running their own business here? That was a step in the right direction. "For themselves? To spend?"

Abigail's snigger of laughter caught me off guard. "You're funning me." She shook her head in disbelief. "Women can't get what their husbands don't give them. Everything goes to CPRC. The Church. It gets apportioned out based on need and other things." Her voice faltered at that moment as though "other things" might just be a bit of a thorn in her side.

"Abigail, you need to get Jenny back to one of the lines here. I doubt that little blister will keep her from putting in a full day's work." Marybeth's hostility embraced Abigail with the same distaste she had shown for me. Her narrow face with oversized brown eyes and a pendulous lower lip reminded me of a sulky llama.

Whatever I had done to her didn't have anything to do with the Sion Soap factory. She was in a bellicose mood. Mr. Darken's friend Maylene had baked me an angel food cake for my birthday. Marybeth hadn't even offered me a Band-Aid.

CHAPTER 7

B y the time the black Chrysler pulled up in front of the so-called Industrial Science Academy, I had graduated from the lye and cold-water line to the cutting and wrapping area. Considering my hostile expression, no one in the room would let me near a vat of boiling oil.

Bone-tired, I plopped down next to Lorena in the back seat. She had the lively air of a child who has spent a good day in the classroom.

"Do you know that the ancient prophets of our church lived in America 600 years before Christ was born?"

"America wasn't America until Columbus misidentified it in 1492. Before that, the Vikings were here. And, before that the Native Americans following wooly mammoths. You must have misunderstood the teacher." I dismissed the history lesson and closed my tired and stinging eyes so I didn't have to see the chimpanzee neck of Mr. Darken.

He swung his head around. "Lorena is absolutely right. *The Book of Mormon* contains the Word of

Wisdom passed down to us by Joseph Smith in 1833. Your understanding of history is sadly compromised by public education, Jenny." The eyes watching me in the rearview mirror expected a response. I fought the impulse to roll my eyes.

The bait didn't hook me. It did Lorena.

"I like to be right. Jenny is always right. This time I'm right." The glee in Lorena's voice made me want to stuff a sock in her mouth. I should have.

"And what's more, we didn't come from apes and monkeys like you said, Jenny. We came from Adam. He was the first man and then girls got carved out of his rib."

This time, Mr. Darken turned around and beamed a big, toothy porcelain-capped smile—same teeth as Elder Bonner. Apparently, the Elders and Apostles could afford better dental care than their wives and children. "You listened and learned so well that when we get to the Retreat, I'll see that your mother gives you a nice after-school snack."

I maintained my after-school silence. I wanted only one thing when we got to that icky chalet in the woods—at least half an hour, more if I could wangle it.

I did by dangling my blistered hand in front of Mr. Darken. A translucent marble, puffy with fluid looked worse than it actually was. "I need to go for a run. I'm totally out of training. I get very disagreeable when I can't take out my frustration by running. I can show this to Mother and tell her how I got injured on caustic lye in your Academy. Or go for a run and keep quiet."

"Stay within sight of the Compound. Don't even think about going through the fence. You'll be fried blacker than that sausage you cooked me this morning." He turned, flung an arm around Lorena's shoulders, and the two of them stepped along like Fred and Ginger.

From the porch of the chalet, he shouted almost gleefully: "There's grizzlies, black bear, and wolves in the woods—a city girl probably never got chased by one of those. I doubt you can run that fast."

Lorena faltered on the steps and grabbed his hand. She thought wolves were friendly as Lassie, but she had an unholy fear of bears.

I HAD DONE almost six kilometers, my floral skirt sticking to my legs like adhesive as I paced myself down the gravel road, slowing down as I passed one and two-story houses, some with lights shining behind very clean windows to ward off the early night. It was just an ordinary subdivision of family houses in a remote corner of Idaho. So why was I so jittery?

By the time I got to Zion Chapel, the setting sun splashed against two narrow, stained-glass windows, spraying welcoming light. I stopped to check out the nearest window with a crude image of what appeared to be Jesus and a lamb. I stepped up to the porch and squinted.

Splinters of bright glass formed a near facsimile of a bearded man in a white robe. Draped around his neck was something resembling a vintage fox stole with beady black eyes.

Just as I burst out in uncontrollable giggling, I heard the sound of a piano. It wasn't playing "Onward Christian Soldiers." Bach Inventions were chasing across the keys in contrapuntal fashion.

My father and I kept Bach on for background music when we worked on old clocks. "Orderly. Brilliantly mechanical. Perfect music for fixing clocks." I could hear his voice as clear as the music inside.

The pain of remembering brought tears to my eyes. Struggling with betrayal, I should never have gotten into that Chrysler in Portland. I should have screamed the house down. That would probably have landed me in some bureaucratic Child Services place while Mr. Darken made off with Mother and Lorena.

At least I was here. And able to run. My internal clock told me I was fast, in spite of uneven terrain. I did some quick stretches and tiptoed up the church steps. The door was slightly ajar. I eased inside and saw Josh Barnes bent over the piano, the perfect spheres of his shoulders taxing the fabric of his shirt. I could imagine dimples where the tendons clung to the bone.

The current that ran through my body started when my breasts brushed the back of the pew and zipped on down to somewhere in my belly then down and down.

The severity of the shock depends on the path through your body. That's why a bird can sit on a high voltage wire with both feet and not fry. I was frying on a perfectly calm day when not a crackle of electricity splintered the sky.

"You can come closer, Jenny Hatchet. I don't like being spied on."

"I wasn't . . . uh . . . I recognized Bach. My father and I listened to the same thing you're playing. He really liked that music."

"Mine too. He played the piano in church. Mrs. Hodges does it now. She sings OK, but she bangs out hymns like she's playing at a honky-tonk. I can't stand to listen."

He flashed a descending arpeggio down the keyboard and spun around on the stool. "Did Mr. Darken let you out of prison?"

"He let me go for a run. I convinced him." I tried to keep an impassive expression on my face, but Josh was moving down the aisle toward me. His eyes were a fathomless blue; he moved as though he were still hearing music, his old boat shoes making a pleasing rhythm against the sandstone floor.

"Convinced?" Just the hint of a grin wrinkled the corners of his eyes. "Comes from the Latin. Means to conquer or overcome. I don't think that describes your relationship with Mr. Darken." His mouth remained in a perfectly straight line.

"What about outwitted? Persuasion? AKA Jane Austen." The only Latin I could remember was *memento mori* from a tombstone adjacent to my father's grave. I didn't want to remember death. Who would put that on a tombstone? But, I thought I might impress Josh with the scope of my reading.

"I prefer *Emma*. She's meddlesome to a fault and gets away with it. Puts her nose where it doesn't belong on purpose. Determination is a good quality, don't you think?"

"I guess so, but I just want to . . ." I plucked at layers of damp daisy fabric clinging to my legs and stuttered like a ninny.

"To what?" I could almost feel his soft breath on my neck although he stood a foot away from me.

I didn't dare tell him what I was determined to do. Get the hell out of Dodge. No matter how good he looked, he was one of them. A bred and born CPRCer. He probably believed that Mormons—not Pilgrims—greeted the Native Americans or walked hand in hand with them over the Bering Strait. But, his interest might be worth a veiled query.

"I understand how you people like living out here. Beautiful scenery. No hassle from the neighbors. I grew up in Portland. I'd like to finish high school there; then maybe go to a university close to . . ." I couldn't finish the lie. I didn't want to be within half a continent of where Mr. Darken lived. "Where do the kids go after they finish school here?" I asked brightly, but fearful of the answer.

"They don't."

"Don't what?"

"Finish high school. They might get what amounts to an eighth grade education. Some go to trade school to be mechanics. Mostly, the boys end up as farmers like their fathers, like Enoch Bonner. Some just leave. No place for them here."

Well. That was the most hopeful thing I'd heard.

"Like cashiered out of the ranks? Sent off to live with relatives?" That didn't sound bad to me though I didn't even know I had a relative until Mother let it slip at my father's funeral that he had a brother named Hal. Hal Hatchet. Nice assonance in that name. My missing uncle.

"More like booted out if they don't have a place. The Elders and Apostles like to keep the ratio lopsided."

I had no idea what he meant, but from the expression on Josh's face, he'd said too much.

"The girls I meant. What do they do besides make soap and sew?"

"Milk cows. Work in the fields. Get married. Have babies." The sly expression he flashed at me faded instantly.

"You're going to get in trouble if anyone sees you talking to me, Jenny. And, trouble you can't even imagine will come down on me—and my mother. After my father died, my mother said three words: 'We will endure.' We have. My father was the accountant for our businesses here. He taught me spreadsheets, how to make myself useful on the computer. Nobody bothers me much—unless you count Enoch. He's a bloody nuisance, but I mostly avoided him. Until you came along."

He brushed past me and exited the church. I kept hearing his last words "until you came along" like some kind of romantic refrain. Something Michael Buble might sing. Something I might remember for a long time if he sang it.

THE THREESOME AROUND the table weren't waiting dinner for me. "Cheese n' Mac, your favorite," Mother twitted; she was chirpy as a caged budgie, her untouched plate betraying her anxiety. Mr. Darken glowered at me.

It was the only home-cooked dish that Mother couldn't turn into a disaster—unless al dente pasta wasn't your thing. I scooted into the empty chair and spooned a soggy lump onto my plate as Mr. Darken continued to watch me balefully.

Determined to make this a normal we're-all-together-around-the-table meal, Mother launched into an account of her day with Mrs. Barnes.

"We spent most of the morning on the history of your people, Gomer. That Joseph Smith was quite an amazing teenager. Jesus visited him when he was only fourteen. Jenny, do you know that he was given solid gold tablets from the lost tribe of Israel?" She looked at me expectantly as I silently shoveled in stiff macaroni.

"Odd that he seemed to have misplaced the tablets." She glanced down at the thin band on her finger, probably wondering if it was plated. "I guess gold back then wasn't bringing over a thousand an ounce like it is today."

Mr. Darken didn't appear to be following her train of thought and had begun paring his nails with an oversized pocketknife. At the dinner table! We all stopped eating and stared at him. Mother broke the ice.

"Mrs. Barnes seems like a very *refined* lady." The fingernail paring continued. "She told me she's a widow with a teenage son. Being so recently widowed myself, I thought I could offer some sympathy and tried to draw her out. She said her husband was found in the pen with a dairy bull. Gored and trampled almost past recognition. That poor boy of hers found him."

She now had the attention of both Lorena and me. I knew that Lorena was thinking about how to stay far away from mad bulls in the dairy barn. I was wondering if Josh acted so testy because of that terrible experience.

Mr. Darken popped the blade of his knife closed. "Bad accidents happen on farms. It's the nature of the business."

I was nothing if not quick on the uptake. "I thought Josh Barnes's father was an accountant." I should have bitten my tongue. Josh had told me that when we were talking in the Chapel less than an hour earlier.

Retribution was not long in coming. "God gives some of us different kinds of talents, but he expects all of us to labor in the fields."

"Or in Soap Academy." I just couldn't let him have the last word.

The blank expression on Mother's face told me that she had no idea where I'd spent my day. As she opened her mouth, I had a sinking feeling that she and I suffered from the same hoof and mouth disease.

"As I was saying, I felt sorry for Mrs. Barnes as she told me about the . . . manner . . . of her husband's death. What I didn't fully understand was something else she said. Her son who was only seventeen then was moved to the SYM facility the day after his father's funeral."

"SYM?" I asked.

"Living quarters for single young men. They don't live with their families after they reach a certain age. But it seems very harsh to separate a mother and son who had just experienced such a tragedy." Mother looked inquisitively across the table at Mr. Darken as he attacked cold macaroni and cheese with new fervor.

I made a careful little church and steeple with the people tucked inside and angled the hand with a nasty blister toward my mother, hoping she would notice her daughter's injury. She didn't. She just patted Mr. Darken's hand as though he was the one with the injury.

Time for another foray onto the battlefield of the dinner table. "Sounds like the Spartans," I said. He didn't respond.

Trying again. "In Sparta, if a child were born weak or sickly, they tossed it off a cliff. They took all the boys when they were seven years old and put them in military-style barracks and trained them to endure pain and to fight."

"We are a peaceful people. You have a smart mouth, Jenny. I suggest you take it to bed. I've had a long day and need relaxation." The come-hither smile that Mr. Darken flashed toward my mother was met with a confused expression. Mother had an uneasy sense that something wasn't quite right in this new family.

It wasn't. Lorena spotted it immediately. "You get under Mr. Darken's skin, Jenny. You do it on purpose." She tucked her hand into mine as we headed toward our bedroom. "Mrs. Maylene told him that I hemmed two dish cloths in class today and catch on fast. He was that pleased." She beamed up at me.

"What do you mean you hemmed dish cloths? In school?" I asked. Lorena's peal of laughter rang out. "Of course. It's what they call the useful arts. We have reading, arithmetic, and Bible study in the morning—then we are learning to sew in the afternoon. My first big project will be a dress that doesn't look like this." Lorena pinched the coarse floral fabric of her droopy skirt.

"Your first big project" I muttered between clenched teeth "will be to learn something that wasn't written on disappearing tablets of gold." I thought it best not to mention that Joseph Smith Jr. was a maniacal polygamist. As in the case of Mother, ignorance might help Lorena remain in Mr. Darken's good graces until I came up with a plan.

Unable to find anything but an out-of-date *Farmer's Almanac* and *The Book of Mormon* in this house, I had to do a geography lesson from memory on sheets of plain paper that I had found in a kitchen drawer. I drew a hasty map of the United States and sketched in the shapes of states as well I could remember where they fit.

Lorena spotted Florida, Texas, California and Nevada. The rest were sort of jumbled up in the middle. "Here's where we are—Idaho. We're way up here in this corner. And there's Oregon."

Lorena measured the space with her forefinger. "We're really close to home. I expect Mother will get tired of Mr. Darken being so bossy, and we'll go back to Portland." She looked up at me with a sly grin. "Mr. Darken promised to take me on a horse Saturday if I keep doing good in school." She tossed aside the map we'd struggled to make. "I hope Mother won't plan to leave before then."

Not to worry. Mother was not a long-range planner. Unfortunately, Lorena had inherited her short attention span.

CHAPTER 8

Sion Soap rarely had such a passionate stirrer. I practiced French verbs in my head as I agitated the lye. *Tuer, mutiler, battre*—I wound down from capital crimes to felonies. After a morning on the lye-into-cold-water detail, goggled and gloved this time, I dropped exhausted onto a chair in the corner of the room.

Abigail, who had been on the wrapping and labeling detail, eased herself down beside me and handed me a thick sandwich, ham on whole wheat bread. "I hope you don't mind visiting with me, Jenny." She darted a glance at the women sitting like a cabal around the table in the opposite corner.

"The women are shunning me. It was my own fault that I got moved here away from the sewing I absolutely love; I'm a very good seamstress." Her green eyes dropped with a sense of shame, as though she'd been booted out of an atelier, dropped from the ranks of haute couture.

"If you're good and you like sewing, why would they send you here to make soap?"

"Punishment. I walked out with Zeb MacAfee." Her voice was so hushed I could hardly hear her.

"So . . . ?" I drawled out my response in what I hoped was a soothing manner. Walking with someone named Zeb sounded like an innocent pastime. Abigail's cheeks flared to match her ginger hair. Her fingers beat a nervous tattoo on the back of my chair.

"I'm promised to Jeremiah Winner, Elder Winner's son." Abigail flushed again—and not with pleasure.

"I thought Elder Bonner was the head honcho here. Who is Elder Winner?" The hierarchy of priests in this place was beginning to confound me.

"We have several elders in this ward. I'm surprised that Mr. Darken didn't have you study with Mrs. Barnes before coming out. That's usually the way it works."

"Josh Barnes's mother?"

"Yes. I used to . . . to . . ."

"To what?"

"Fancy him. When we were young kids. All the girls did. He doesn't like girls. He doesn't like anyone." Abigail huffed slightly with frustration. "All I did was walk down to the pond and back with Zeb. It was daylight. One of Elder Winner's wives saw me."

"One of his what?" At the moment I let out a shriek, the lights went out. The creaky overhead fans sputtered to a stop, and a voice screamed: "Don't anyone move until I get the door open for some light. They's vats of hot lard everywheres."

A feeble ray of afternoon light outlined the angular body of Marybeth in the doorway. In her hand was an industrial-sized flashlight. "You girls, Abigail and Jenny. Make yourselves useful. See if you can get them two windows on the back wall unstuck. Just feel your way along the wall."

They were old crank-out, metal-framed windows like we had in the gym in our high school in Portland. I knew their temperament. I whacked one paint-clogged fastener and whipped the window into obedience. The other one was past salvaging.

With the additional faltering light, I could see Marybeth over by the box, flipping and flipping. Obviously, she did not know what she was doing. I eased on around the wall, skirting the tubs of hot grease, and came up behind her. By now, all the women had crowded in to watch her pop one switch and then another.

"Probably a fuse." Like a flock of geese the women turned in unison and stared at me. "A fuse. Wires break in those old ceramic fuses all the time." I might as well have been speaking Swahili. They acted as though I hadn't spoken a word, or if I had, it was spoken out of place.

"We're already behind on orders. That last batch will have to be done over and cured if we don't get some light in here. I'm afraid to touch this panel again. I saw some flashes. Electricity is dangerous. Someone go find Elder Grund." Marybeth barked an order for anyone who cared to follow it.

"Elder Bonner took Elder Grund to Spokane early this morning to see his heart doctor," Abigail whispered.

"My mother gave them a list in case they finished up early and could pick up supplies."

"Well. I'm not touching that thing again. I've tripped circuit breakers before, but I don't know a thing about electricity beyond that. I guess we could get some kerosene lamps; without those overhead fans, we'll bake in here with all those burners going full blast."

"I can fix it." My voice rang out with more confidence than I really felt. I had helped my father replace half a dozen old fuse boxes. Why anyone would have one with these old ceramic fuses made no sense. Much better technology had been out for years.

Marybeth waved the flashlight like a strobe light on a dance floor until it settled on my face. "Jenny Hatchet. Town girl. You can't even stir water without burning yourself."

"Maybe not, but I know fuse boxes and circuit breakers and resisters and capacitors and transformers and . . ."

"And how to show off. *You and your mother* sure know that." The anger in Marybeth's voice was not the least suppressed and seemed to have nothing to do with a blackout.

"Give her the flashlight, Marybeth. Let's see if she can do what she says."

Marybeth thrust the flashlight in my hand as though it was a jackhammer and she was on the nether end of it. I aimed it into the fuse box. This one was ancient, probably scavenged from an old building for reuse. If I were lucky, a twist of wire would be stuck into the frame for replacement when the wire in the fuses broke. That's how the electricians used to do it—so they didn't have to look for matching wire.

There it was in a neat coil in the bottom of the box. I angled the heavy flashlight and tried to pull out the top ceramic fuse. I needed both hands. "Abigail. Can you hold the flashlight? These fuses are practically glued into their sockets. I wonder why they haven't all gone bad. Can someone hit the switches on the fans and lights off until I'm finished here?"

Abigail moved over near me and held the flashlight with trembling hands. "Electricity scares me, Jenny. I saw three of our cows fall over when lightning hit the fence in the pasture. Fire was shooting out of them. I swear it was."

"Yeah. Lightening can be powerful. Tell you what. Just hold on to the person next to you and she can do the same and the one on the end gets the jolt." My harsh laugh was meant to cover my ineptness in getting the fuses out.

"This one. See the broken wire. Who has a screwdriver and wire cutters? Scissors will work."

Marybeth rustled around in a drawer under one of the tables and came back over with a flimsy screwdriver and sturdy scissors. I needed my own tools. This would have to do. I rotated the screws at both ends, pulled out the wire, clipped off a length of new wire, and anchored both ends with the screws. I pushed it firmly into place and flipped the breaker again.

"Turn on the wall switches." Marybeth stood rooted to her spot like some ancient guardian of the fuse box.

Two of the other women trotted over to the wall. Light flooded the room. The overhead fans stirred the steamy air around.

Almost as quickly as the steam drifted out the open door and window, the very air I was breathing seemed lighter, cleaner, friendlier. Three of the women patted me on the back. One shook my hand. Two sent tentative smiles my way as I stirred soap for forty-five minutes, until it looked like sickly vanilla pudding and could be poured into a plastic-lined cardboard box.

When we took a break, the guard of the women had dropped. A few of them watched me as though I were some kind of alien species, but one of them handed me a glass of well water and another passed the plate of oatmeal cookies to me before she offered it to others.

In spite of these small gestures, I kept thinking that I was such a misfit. Always had been. But here, *a stranger in a strange land*. Heinlein's book about the human born and raised in Mars before he came back to Earth kept popping into my head as I looked into faces of these women. Baggy eyes, baggy clothes, baggy lives— all of them old before their time, used up by this place.

The chunks of an oatmeal cookie went flying out of my mouth when the light came on in my head. Abigail had mentioned it—quite without noticing that she had said something really terrible. "One of Elder Winner's wives saw me."

That's what made it even more terrible. A girl takes a walk with a boy she likes and is sent to the soap factory as punishment—a judgment Abigail believed she deserved. Abigail didn't even falter when she said: "One of Elder Winner's wives saw me."

Like one of those coy revelations that mystery writers use before they surprise the reader at the end of the story, I felt the weight of *deus ex machina* plummeting out of heaven onto my head, as though the gods had already dropped enough hints and needed to bludgeon me with the truth.

Maylene and Marybeth did Mr. Darken's bidding for a reason. They didn't have last names for a reason. The reason was us. More particularly, the reason was my mother, my foolish, duped mother. I spotted Marybeth as she marched up behind me, primed as a Roman general to give me another order.

"Stuff it, Marybeth." The rules of respect for older people had just flown out of that dirty window I had cranked open earlier. "You're not my mother. Quit bossing me around. I know what needs to be done here. Not everyone is as stupid as you think."

Abigail grabbed my arm and pulled me away. "Oh, Jenny. You should never talk like that to one of . . ." Her ashen face looked sickly against her bright hair. "She'll find a way to get even. They always do."

I was certain that she would. But I would keep my distance in the soap factory. When that long, llama face screwed up in anger, I didn't intend to be within spitting distance—or near a vat of hot grease.

CHAPTER 9

Sitting on a stoop outside the Sion Soap Factory when you're primed for action is as E.F. Benson says "tarsome." Everyone had left the soap factory. I thought about taking off for a nice run back to the Retreat, but Marybeth growled at me. "You better wait for him if you know what's good for you."

A light breeze lifted heavy branches of the Douglas firs, melting the dense shadows around them. A tractor furrowed a field in the distance. Two women gathered laundry from a clothesline, moving methodically from the end poles toward the center, as though engaged in a stylized dance.

I imagined how a painter might look upon this scene—smoke wafting up from the tops of houses, people going about the ordinary tasks of country living.

That same mystery painter might catch me skirting closer than necessary to where I could see Josh outside a long, low building splitting logs into kindling. The painter might see me noticing how perfectly orchestrated Josh's body was as he bent and struck and bent and struck again. A painter might just catch that eager expression on my face.

Sherlock's voice sounded in my ear as he talked to Watson about what might appear to be the unspoiled beauty of the countryside. "Think of the deeds of hellish cruelty, the hidden wickedness which may go on year in, year out, in such a place, and none the wiser."

The painting in my head shifted to a close-up of Mr. Darken's face as he drove up, dark as a Mohawk with anger. It wasn't directed at me, and he was unusually garrulous, talking in a friendly way as I climbed into the front seat of the pickup.

"There's a weak place in the electric fence. Marybeth told me you know about electrical equipment—and being disrespectful." I waited for the lecture that didn't come as he ground the gears, looking for reverse.

"The Kootenai got out of its banks yesterday. Most of the men are out trying to keep the creek from washing out spring wheat. I had no help at all with that mess this afternoon." An air of sanctimony settled about him as he flashed me a put-upon look. The "mess" to which he was referring wasn't my little set-to with Marybeth.

Self-righteousness flooded over me like the ancient Nile. This bigamist couldn't imagine the mess I was planning for his life—jail time leading the list. I'd spring it when the time was right. Disarm the enemy. I put on my interested-in-what-you've-got-to-say face. He took the hook.

"Our big Hereford bull got through the electric fence to the heifers. Ever since Cyrus Grund started having these little bouts with his heart, the fencing around here is going to hell in a hand basket."

"Did the bull gore them or something?" I flashed on an image of Josh finding his bleeding father under the hooves of a dairy bull.

Mr. Darken snorted. "Or something!" He looked over at me with an interest that made me squirm. "You don't know anything about cattle, do you Jenny?"

Affirmative. And I didn't want to know more than how to select a steak with good marbling.

"Hereford bulls don't gore. Dairy bulls might." He blinked as though the same bad image of Josh's father had popped into his head. "We weight the Herefords' horns down so they can't do any damage. The heifers that got . . ." he paused as though he might be editing his script. "That got interfered with today have never had calves. If we breed them first to one of our small Mexican bulls, they have smaller calves. Less risk. Easier on everyone."

Well. I certainly got that. Biology was never my strong suit, but I had paid attention to the chapter on repro-duction. So much so that my next words shot out of my mouth like a geyser: "What do you mean everyone? It's the poor little heifer that will have a monster calf."

"Snow hits here early. If you'd ever pulled a calf in a snowstorm, you'd . . ." He stopped. "Men's work mostly. Costly to lose the cow and the calf. I finally got the bull into the corral. After he was out of and into the chute so to speak." He choked back a vulgar chuckle and slammed the pickup into another gear.

Mr. Darken gave me what he considered an apology. "So I'm late. Maylene took Lorena home over an hour ago. We got to do something about that fence though. Figure out why the current is weak in that section.

"That big Hereford split that fence like it didn't have a charge in it. Someone should have been paying attention. Those heifers have been sidling up to that end of the fence all week. Tempting the bull. That's why he broke through." I assumed there was some kind of message here for me considering the pontifical tone of his voice. The old wool hat he was wearing peaked at the top like a bishop's miter.

The thought of that great, huffing bull terrified me. I had jogged along the side of the fence, confident that the electric current would protect me. That bull deserved a cage for what he'd done to those young cows. I could fix that fence so it wouldn't happen again. When he came sniffing and slobbering up to that wire, he'd get a jolt that would knock him to his knees. Too bad I couldn't wire off all the male Saints.

This one driving the pickup would get a jolt himself when I decided just where and when I'd drop my bombshell.

MOTHER STOOD BY the kitchen sink—Eve balancing a glossy apple on the tips of her fingers. Like a carnival professional, she flipped the paring knife in her other hand so that it flashed end over end in the direction of Mr. Darken's throat—before it fell with a clatter onto the cabinet.

"You two startled me." A disarming smile settled on her face. "I have a meat loaf in the oven and a pie almost ready to bake."

For someone whose idea of a home-cooked dessert was re-pinching the edge of a frozen store-bought pie, Mother's announcement of dinner in the oven surprised me almost as much as the thought that she might really disembowel Mr. Darken with a paring knife. She had cause. Would have cause when I revealed the secrets of his harem.

"You are baking a pie?"

"Mrs. Barnes made the two crusts and the meatloaf, but I'm putting it together. A really nice meal for my family."

Lorena, who was dumping half a shaker of cinnamon on the apples, stopped to squeak out: "Two more dish towels today, Mr. Darken. I guess that means a horseback ride."

I guess that means a ride back to Portland on the first bus heading west. I had mastered not only speaking but thinking with a forked tongue. The setting was right considering the woman holding an apple and that old bull of a man who had just taken a huge bite out of the evil side of it. GOD had no idea that knowledge was about to light up his world.

"I'll be back in a minute to help, Mother. Just need to do a couple of things first." *Like packing my old clocks and tools in a pillowcase.* The Barbie bag could stay behind. We would eat Mrs. Barnes's food before we left—it would be a long night on the bus. It seemed a kindness to Josh to show appreciation for his mother's cooking. I wouldn't be telling him goodbye. The police would probably take us somewhere to file charges, and then to a bus headed home to Portland.

"This meatloaf is special." Mr. Darken reached across Lorena's plate to slice off a second slab. "Better than Marybeth's. She does fix good venison stew though. Remember? She and Maylene made us that honeymoon dinner when we first got here. Obliging of them." Gormlessly, he leaned over his plate to shovel in another mouthful.

If I had Huang Lee's heirloom sword, I'd have swatted his fat head off his hunkered-over body and kicked it all the way down the stairs of this harem called the Retreat.

The icy voice piercing this little family get-together sounded exactly like mine: "Do Maylene and Marybeth always respond to your perfidy with special dinners for new brides?"

Mother was the first to interject a retort. "Really, Jenny. What a thing to say. I don't even know what 'perfidy' means, but it doesn't sound like a nice word."

"How about treachery? Or faithlessness? Or violating wedding vows? Or having at least three wives at the same time? Take your pick, Mother."

Mr. Darken bent over, gasped, and clutched his throat—that might be a good sign that the raw sausage parasites were working on his aorta. When he sat up, his face was the color of beet soup.

"Adam fell that men might be, and men are, that they might have joy."

His voice sounded heavy. No wonder. It was probably weighted with guilt. He'd be ticking off the years he'd spend in prison for bigamy—and regretting ever taking a bite of that apple from my mother's hand.

He picked up my mother's limp hand. "You bring me joy, Clara. You and little Lorena."

His voice was soft, but I could see an odd flickering deep in Mr. Darken's eyeballs, as though he was scanning the pages of a book looking for the good parts. Then the lights went out. The expression on his face was one of repulsion. I thought he might be mirroring my repulsion. He wasn't. I had ceased to figure in this so-called family equation.

"I was married to Maylene when I was just eighteen years old, a boy really. Her pa and mine arranged it. Maylene had a breeder's body, wide hips, and so on. After four years when she didn't take, Pa had to arrange another marriage."

Mr. Darken's thumb was making odd little circles on Mother's lifeless hand as though initiating a mating ritual—like one of those weird insects that appear to be rubbing but are really sucking out their mate's bodily fluids.

"Marybeth didn't take either. But, they're both good, Christian women." There was a certain, plaintive whine about his words that was even more disgusting than the words themselves.

Mother had not said a word nor removed her limp hand from that of Mr. Darken. Lorena had both fists crammed against her mouth, as though she would never find enough thumbs for comfort.

That gruesome nursery rhyme popped into my head: "Who killed Cock Robin? Who saw him die? Who caught his blood? Who'll dig his grave? Who'll toll the bell? All I could remember was that the bull offered to toll the bell—the bull because he could pull. Pull the wool over someone's eyes.

"You're sealed to my wives, the same as me, Clara. They call each other sisterwives. That's what a Celestial Marriage means. We'll all be together in heaven, sealed for eternity. Lorena will be sealed to us too. Or we can keep that for later."

When GOD said "later," an image of a teenage Lorena swathed in white satin flashed before me. Edward was not waiting at the altar with his fangs dripping blood. Mr. Darken with his big, square incisors had replaced him.

"Out of here, Mother! I'm packed. You and Lorena just need to grab your coats. I saw a phone on the wall of the soap building. We can use that to call a taxi." I was playing it low-key. My intent was to dial 911 for the police.

No one moved. Lorena's breathing came in staccato gasps. A full-blown asthma attack seemed in the offing.

His next words were to my frightened sister. "You'll have three mothers now, Lorena. Maylene always wanted a little girl. We're going to move over to my main house tonight. It's just as well that we all learn to get along under the same roof."

Mother reached into her pocket. I hoped she had stashed a knife or found a gun. The image of Mr. Darken stabbed or gut shot, his blood spraying out like a fire hydrant, brought a sense of pride that I hadn't felt for my mother in a long time.

She pulled out Lorena's nebulizer and flipped it across the table. "Go with Jenny, Lorena. Get your things together. I need to talk to Mr. Darken. It seems that I've done something terribly wrong."

My mother reminded me of Hawthorne's Hester as she trod mechanically down the hall—not up to the scaffold where they'd pin the scarlet letter for adultery on her chest. Mother looked as though she had accepted the big letter "A" but might have a thing or two to say about it. I still held out hope that Mother would surprise me.

I could see Mr. Darken thumbing a cell phone as he followed her. I didn't know he had one. I could dial 911 on that if I could get my hands on it.

The screams and shouts coming from the red room should have caused the neighbors to report domestic abuse, but we had no neighbors. The ugly little chalet was far from the main compound. I rummaged through my tool bag and found a big screwdriver for Lorena to hold as a weapon and a hammer that I would relish burying in the skull of Mr. Darken.

An eerie silence settled like thick fog around us. I remembered the white ropes in the chest. Mr. Darken had probably gagged and tied up Mother. Lorena and I would be next. "Get on your coat, Lorena. We may need to make a run for it." I hissed at her.

"I'll have to stop by Mrs. Maylene's house to get my kitten. She's got one for me. She told me today. Mother says animals cause my asthma. I don't think so. We'll take the kitten with us to Portland. I guess I won't have a horseback ride after all."

CHAPTER 10

I loved my little sister too much to choke her on the spot. But, the impulse was very strong. "We need to get out of here with Mother now! Mr. Darken might get those men, those Elders and Apostles, to be on his side. Keep that screwdriver pointed straight ahead and stand by the front door. I'll get him with this hammer if I get a chance. I need to check on Mother."

The red room door was ajar. Mother was prettily dissolved into tears on the bed. Mr. Darken was on his knees at the side of the bed repeating his mantra: "It is not sin. Service to wives is obligation, not sin. Now, I want you, only you, Clara. We are married in the eyes of God. You are safe here from the evil of the world. I will protect you and your girls from the evil of the world."

I seemed to be peeking in the crack of the door at the evil of the world, on his knees, sermonizing as though there was no tomorrow.

The sharp crack of the front door burst like a gunshot.

"You girls get yourselves into the car. It's time we stopped this tomfoolery and settled down like the family God intends us to be. Under one roof. *His.*" Marybeth's gnarly thumb pointed down the hall toward the red room.

I hefted my small ball peen hammer. It wasn't worth a damn unless I could make a surprise attack from above on a fragile skull. The two women blocking the front door looked anything but fragile.

Maylene had the exhausted appearance of a flattened balloon, drooping behind Marybeth. Like an on-point hunting dog, Marybeth was sniffing the wind for helpless birds.

The sparrow among us dropped her screwdriver and flung herself into the arms of Maylene.

The biceps slicer that Marybeth locked onto me hyper rotated my elbow joint until I screeched in pain and dropped the hammer on her toe. "You'll pay for that, missy." As she goose-stepped me down the hall to my bedroom, she barked orders.

"Maylene, you get the young-un's clothes and grab that pie that's cooling on the counter. No need to waste food. This one needs all my attention." Marybeth eyed the empty Barbie suitcase on my bed. "Put that pillow-case of stuff in this. Easier to haul with rollers."

"You take it, Marybeth. Consider it a birthday present. It suits you," I said snidely, comparing her bushy locks with Barbie's golden coif. The gift didn't reduce the pressure on my arm. Marybeth just might make it on the Olympic wrestling team with very little training.

As I huddled next to a sniveling Lorena in the backseat of the Chrysler, I thought about Mother alone with that licentious man, purring like a tomcat as he explained away his sins.

Before Marybeth assaulted me, I had watched Mother's face, awash in baptismal tears, listening. She was *actually* listening to him, arms rigid, body tense, but hearing his confession.

The low voice of Maylene drifted into the backseat like an afterthought. "Women of our religion don't marry for love. They marry for duty."

Well. If those words were meant as a comfort, she could save her little homilies. As sure as there was a real God in a real Heaven, Gomer Obadiah Darken would die unshriven and plunge straight down to Hell. I'd do everything I could to speed him on his way. I wrapped my arms around Lorena and tried to think about how things had gone so wrong as Marybeth steered the car around potholes.

IT WASN'T REALLY Mother's fault. She was who she was. If she had been a professional woman—a teacher, an accountant, or even one of those tight-assed corporate women in pencil skirts and pointy shoes—our lives would have gone on in spite of the fact that Daddy's life ended too soon. Same school. Same neighborhood. Bills paid. Future assured. We'd just soldier on with an empty place around the table.

I thought of the weeping woman back in the red room—just like Picasso's "Weeping Woman," her face thalo green, her jaws violet with pain. No matter how intense the pain, it would dissipate when the sun came up, and all the streaks of tears will have dried.

My mother is so pretty that strangers smile at her and so helpless that she plants daffodil bulbs upside down. I promised Daddy that I would always look after her and Lorena. I promised years before he took a detour into the McKenzie River. I didn't know how hard promises were to keep.

As Marybeth eased the car down a gravel road into the main part of the Compound, I counted fifteen houses in a kind of extended semi-circle with dim porch lights. The backs of the houses were cluttered with small sheds that backed up to an open field. From across the field, I could see a similar cluster of houses.

The permanent residence of the extended Darken family loomed before us like a beached square-rigger, horizontal boards running the length of it and not a sail in sight. The porch light punctuated the darkness in a distinctly unwelcome manner.

"For now, you and Lorena will share a bedroom upstairs. Mine's upstairs too. Maylene as first wife has the bedroom closest to the kitchen, warmer." I caught just a hint of spite in Marybeth's tone. "Your mother will have the room off to the right with the parlor next to it."

I didn't dare ask about Mr. Darken's bedroom. An image of him as a huge Hawkmoth—the moth with a long proboscis—flitting from bedroom to bedroom made me gasp audibly. That little honeysuckle child I held in my arms in the backseat wiggled because I was holding her so tightly.

Nothing about Mr. Darken's house surprised me. A big, boxy front room held an assortment of mismatched sofas and chairs covered in indestructible scratchy herculon. Mustard daisies marched in exact lines down the wallpaper as though Marybeth had commandeered them to behave.

I read somewhere that people in the Nineteenth Century died breathing vapors from wallpaper—from one of those green paints that William Morris used. William Morris would have swallowed arsenic willingly if he'd been forced to endure this wallpaper.

Hideous arrangements of artificial flowers bunched themselves into every corner of the room. They went well with the vomit green of the kitchen appliances. Marybeth pointed them out admiringly. "Mr. Darken found a good sale in Portland some years back. We had the choice of avocado green or burnt orange. Elder Bonner's wife took the only robin egg blue." The llama's lower lip sagged with disappointment.

To the right, just off the living room, two large double doors blocked off another room. One door hung wide. Marybeth hurried to swing it closed but not before I got a glimpse of a big roll-top desk covered with ledgers and an iMac sitting at a smaller work station. My stolen MacBook was probably in that room. Probably had dial-up connectivity. A slow connection to the outside world, but at least a link.

"Mr. Darken's office. Off limits. No one is allowed in there." Marybeth sounded just like the warden's aide, defining the prison bounds.

Aside from being as cold as pack ice at the North Pole, our bedroom surprised us. A quilt made of blocks of color reminded me of Calder's prints that I liked so much. We collapsed into a mattress of down, so soft that we didn't mind the odd bumps of bed slats beneath it.

"Maylene didn't say a thing about my kitten. She promised this morning." Lorena was nothing if not fixated on the small pleasures she anticipated. She had not mentioned the horseback ride. Mr. Darken had moved further down her list of what to avoid—probably somewhere below mad bulls and evil trolls.

At that moment, the door eased open and a small gray-striped ball of fluff moved on "little cat feet" across the room and sat eying us. In a single fluid movement, Lorena hung off the side of the bed, scooped up the kitten, cupped it next to her face and fell into a sleep that was not troubled at all by asthmatic breathing.

CHAPTER 11

Living under the same roof with Maylene, Marybeth and Mr. Darken made me feel as though I had just moved down to Dante's Eighth Circle, walking in torment with pimps, seducers, and sorcerers. However, we weren't living with snakes and walking in excrement. Quite the contrary. The odor of Pine-Sol overpowered every molecule of nitrogen and oxygen that crept in Marybeth's sealed windows.

By their own peculiar church dictates, the first wife was the chief wife, the decision-maker for work assignments, and the arbitrator between other sisterwives. That seemed fair to me. The first wife was the most maligned, the first one stabbed in the back, the one with the longest memory of slights as each new wife was added.

Maylene didn't appear to see it that way. I'm not sure what she saw or what she thought. She made little lists marked "Duties" and put everyone's name by tasks— except Mr. Darken. He came and went at will. His will.

Marybeth and I went back to the soap factory where my only ally seemed to be Abigail who had once walked with Zeb and was back doing soap duty. We were stocking soap for five months. By mid-June through late August, the soap factory would be used for canning and making jams and jelly to sell at farmers' markets. Under Mrs. Barnes's supervision, Mother was being schooled in passivity and basic cooking.

Lorena went off with Maylene to a small square brick building called a school every morning and came back home in the evening with a new store of odd information—how Noah managed to load natural enemies such as zebras and lions on the same boat by making the sign of peace over their heads and how suffering should be tolerated as the will of God.

Suffering caught the attention of Mother and me at the same time. We were setting the table for dinner, with Marybeth shouting directions like a short order cook, when Lorena came inside, her face tear-stained; she settled into a floral rocker and pulled her knees up under her chin.

The livid stripes hatch marked on her thin legs were too symmetrical to be cat scratches or a tangle with the blackberry bushes out back. Mother, heading toward the table with a large pitcher of fresh well water, halted, and looked down at Lorena without uttering a word.

The words came out of my mouth as I thought of rusty wire fences, whether or not Lorena had a current tetanus shot, and visualized her small, chattering mouth frozen with lockjaw. "How did you get these welts, Lorena?"

She sniffled and looked frightened. I pulled on her legs gently, examining the welts. "They're not deep, but you may need a tetanus shot. What did you get into?"

"A peach tree switch." She looked past Marybeth who had moved into the room and over at Maylene as though hoping for sympathy.

"I did bad. *She* told me no animals can come into the house, but I took Mr. Stripy Pants upstairs when I got home from school. She said a peach tree switch would help me remember." Lorena sniffled again, never once looking at Marybeth.

Without saying a word, Mother lifted the pitcher of water and dumped it squarely on Marybeth's head, releasing the glass pitcher so that it cracked Marybeth on the shoulder and sent a spray of water down the front of Mother's dress, before crashing to the floor in a dozen pieces.

For the moment, I was speechless, watching Mother like Ophelia sink toward the floor in her waterlogged gown. With surprising strength and swiftness, she gathered up Lorena, whose gangling tortured legs hung down almost to the floor. "Don't you ever strike a child of mine again, you . . . you . . . Harpy!"

Well. Mother surprised me. The mythical beast with a woman's head and body and claws of a bird suited Marybeth to a T.

Surprisingly, Marybeth kept silent as Mother walked up the stairs with Lorena, but her skin was the color of eggshells, so pale that her mood flushed beneath the surface of her cheeks like little fireworks tracing erratic paths—a dead giveaway to her anger.

"Don't think that flibbertigibbet mother of yours makes me angry with her little tantrums. Or jealous. Maylene neither. She relieves us." The knowing glance she cast at me embraced me in some kind of conspiracy. I felt dirty. She pointed to the spreading puddle on the floor. "Clean it up."

Marybeth with her peach tree switch had caused the mess. It wasn't fair to make me mop it up. I smiled weakly and mopped. I needed to choose my battles.

So did Maylene. "I think it's best not to bother Gomer with this little fuss," smiling broader than Claudius. I wanted to scream with Hamlet: "One may smile and smile and be a villain." Shakespeare would tax her sensibilities. She'd probably never read anything but the *The Book of Mormon* and an old Sears catalogue.

The notion that child abuse could be translated into a "little fuss" raised my hackles so much that I wanted to smack that bland, self-contained face of Maylene with the dirty mop rag. She was the one who gave Lorena the kitten. She was complicit in whatever rules had been broken.

I remembered something from Machiavelli, that wonderfully twisted and right-on Italian: "Everyone sees what you appear to be, few knew what you really are." For the moment I would hunch over humbly and mop. And then smile and smile. And plot and plot.

Marybeth went back to stirring her pudding. That was her specialty—butterscotch and chocolate puddings, nasty thick things that clung to the roof of the mouth—after trying them once, Mother, Lorena and I had sworn off puddings.

Neither Lorena nor Mother made an appearance at the dinner table. I watched Mr. Darken woofing down the chocolate pudding and smiling broadly at Marybeth.

The dinner discussion topic was apparently Marybeth's favorite and had something to do with the medicinal qualities of pudding. "When your digestion gets out of kilter, Gomer, there's nothing that sets you right faster than one of my puddings."

He nodded and scooped out another helping. "When bowels are not regular, the entire physique demands a remedy." Marybeth eyed Mr. Darken as though she could see right through him. He might have been one of those clear plastic body torsos like we had in biology class with veins and arteries and great looping intestines—full of pudding.

The goopy chocolate pudding had an odd cast to it tonight. At that moment, I thought of a way to give it a different cast. I just had to find the right ingredient. The thought of healthful colon cleansing took on a new meaning when I watched Mr. Darken. I could orchestrate small discomforts in this house while I planned for the big one.

CHAPTER 12

The big one came sooner than I expected on Tuesday. It was late for the Darken family. They went to bed with the chickens—literally. When the coop door on the pen behind the house was closed for the evening, women and children disappeared to their bedrooms.

There was no TV. The only radio was in Mr. Darken's office—along with access to YouTube and zillions of pieces of information that I would happily give up anything but my $80 stash to access. Lorena and I were wearing out our thumbs and the battery on my Nintendo after sundown in our bedroom. Mario and Grand Theft Auto were our entertainment now that the kitten was locked outside.

I heard the clock downstairs chime ten and thought I'd slip down to the kitchen for a glass of milk. This was unpasteurized, whole milk straight from a cow. Really quite good. When I stepped on the bottom tread, I could hear voices coming from Mr. Darken's office. Mr. Darken's was familiar—the other one less so, but I vaguely remembered hearing it before.

"Samuel Barnes was that close to reporting us. Tax evasion to the IRS and stockpiling weapons to the Bureau. His boy is too inexperienced to . . ." The words dropped in volume. " . . . thought being with the other boys might change . . ."

The next words were clear as a bell, and I recognized the speaker. "Josh might know just enough to make him dangerous." It was Elder Bonner—the same man who prayed over my mother and Mr. Darken's "Celestial Sealing," and the father of that cretin Enoch.

I squatted down and inched myself into the corner leading into the kitchen. I dared not take the stairs with both men only a few feet away. Within minutes, the door to Mr. Darken's office opened, and I could see dusty brown shoes with knotted laces poking unpleasantly from beneath black wool pants that had seen better days. The front door slammed, and the ponderous tread of Mr. Darken's feet took him down the hall to my mother's bedroom. I let a shutter drop on that compartment of my brain.

Back upstairs, I snuggled close to Lorena's toasty little body. Her raspy breathing would have kept me awake even if I hadn't been churning over information faster than Marybeth cranked the Daisy churn.

"Stockpiling weapons." What in the world could that mean? All the men and boys in the Compound used guns. Shooting defenseless wild animals was to these men what heroin is to a user: a rush and a high. I knew the CPRC members stockpiled food. Abigail told me by their law they had to prepare for Armageddon.

They had a large cement block generator-powered building with rows and rows of lockers for frozen food. Every household kept a year's supply of canned goods, dried beans, flour, sugar and cornmeal. Maylene had pointed out her system for rotation, each jar, bag, can, and box marked with a color-coded date.

Why the IRS would be interested in these frugal, hard-working people I couldn't imagine. The police, yes. Bigamy is a crime. Having sex with underage girls is a crime. Who knows what else these people might be getting into? Certainly not liquor or drugs.

Just as Lorena groaned, flopped over and crammed an elbow into my left eye socket, it struck me. Mr. Darken had said there were eighty adult members of the CPRC living in this ward—and that didn't count the children. They had fields of crops, cattle and about an acre of those fat snorting pigs in pens where Enoch had tripped me.

Marybeth had let it slip that the soap business was running over "six figures" and "the jams and jellies doing even better." When we were still at the Retreat, Mr. Darken had talked with pride about their new markets for smoked pork and wholesale beef, not to mention the chickens. "Our lumber sales more than doubled last year," he'd announced one night.

I wasn't paying much attention then, but he'd let it slip quite openly. "We should have not-for-profit status for everything being a church and all—been able to write off equipment, like the Chrysler. The Utah bunch threw a ringer to get us disallowed. We see ourselves as part of the larger fold but adhering more to the older doctrines. They've turned a cold shoulder to CPRC. God hasn't."

The absolute assurance of Mr. Darken that the higher power was on his side had startled me. I didn't know much about not-for-profit organizations, but I knew they were tax-exempt. Josh had mentioned that his father was the CPRC accountant—now Josh did the spreadsheets on computers.

The chill in the bed had nothing to do with the temperature. Josh's father might have wandered into the pen of a mad bull by accident. But it sounded as though Elder Bonner suspected that he was ready to blow the whistle to two federal agencies.

I fell into a tortured sleep where Josh Barnes wrapped himself in a red cape and shouted "Olé" over and over to a large Hereford bull with a single horn like a rhino's snout.

THE TENSION AROUND the morning table subsided a bit when Maylene brightly reminded everyone that "tonight is Wednesday Potluck" in the Community Room. Even Mr. Darken cheered up a bit. "We'll take Jenny and Lorena. They can visit with some of the young people."

I noticed that he carefully avoided looking at the scabs forming on Lorena's legs. Mother must have spilled the beans on Marybeth. She was looking particularly sullen this morning.

I had no idea what "potluck" meant and wasn't about to ask. It was enough of an upper to know that we were going out tonight. Out somewhere. With other people. Being around other people used to be a tonic for Mother. Since we had moved into Mr. Darken's house, Mother walked around like a zombie, one of those corpses with no will of its own, under control of a sorcerer.

IN THE CONTROLLED world of the soap factory during the ice-water-or-cold-milk-break-take-your-choice, I quizzed Abigail about the potluck tonight. She seemed excited that I'd be there. "I can point out Zeb MacAfee to you," she said, blushing as though he might be David without his leaf. "My intended will be there too, Jerry Winner. He isn't though." She giggled as though she'd just made a funny joke. Considering the level of humor in this place, I giggled along with her. And stopped with her next jar-dropping information.

"Josh and his mother always come, but he stands in the corner. Never has much to say to anyone. Enoch will be there. He's sweet on you, but I guess you know that. He told everyone about how he helped you up when you fell down by the pig pens."

My jaw was somewhere down close to my ankle-high Converses. "Sweet on you" sounded like a line from one of those 1950's musicals where gay dancers strutted up to simpering girls—wowing them with undisguised crotch thrusts and pirouettes in cowboy boots.

If I wanted to milk Abigail for all the information she might have, I'd better not throttle the cow. She was. A stupid cow. No. She was just a simple-minded, strikingly pretty girl not much older than me but with fewer choices. Attracted to a boy named Zeb but willing to be wed for eternity to someone named Jerry Winner. "Love is one thing; duty is expected." She answered my question of why as blithely as Maylene had when we drove that night to Mr. Darken's residence.

I patted her empty little head with all the kindness I could muster and said quietly: "I'm sure that you are mistaken about Enoch Bonner. He didn't help me up. He tripped me and held me down. There is nothing between us but animosity." I hissed out the last word so that she would know that Cleopatra's asp wasn't the only one with a wicked bite.

Stirring the lye into cold water, pouring that mixture into melted lard, and dumping the whole stinking mess into a mold took it out of me. I was on my best behavior for Marybeth. I didn't want to do anything for her to report to Mr. Darken. The Potluck thing would be a perfect opportunity to warn Josh. He needed to know that the head honcho Elder might know more than he was willing to admit about an accident-prone accountant and his son.

CHAPTER 13

The six of us walked to Zion Chapel, Marybeth and Maylene coupled like a pair of mismatched draft horses, one overfed and one spindly, each with a large hamper of food. Mother and Mr. Darken followed, not arm in arm, though he bumped her meaningfully. Her arms were wrapped around herself like a whalebone corset.

Lorena was doing the Harlem Shake, or her version of it—a free-form wiggling movement to whatever music might still be in her head since Mr. Darken had absconded with her frog radio.

"Groaning with food" was an understatement. Platters of fried chicken, top-hat high chocolate cakes, casseroles with golden cheesy potatoes, home-canned peaches and pears, and loaves of whole-wheat bread covered tables the length of the Community Room. A human conveyor belt of women moved a steady stream of more food from the kitchen area.

There was a perfect opportunity to make it nearer to the table before the line formed until Marybeth's irksome pinch intervened. "Children go last. Don't you have any manners." It wasn't a question. Spotting Josh's mother over near the side door, I shook off Marybeth's hand. "Grease and sugar, Marybeth. Right up your alley, Miss Manners."

Mrs. Barnes waved toward Mother, beckoning her over. As Mother edged uncomfortably around clusters of hostile women and men trying to conceal lascivious glances, I thought of how Jezebel must have felt just before the crowd threw her out of the window to be eaten by dogs. Happily, the windows in the Community Room were only two feet off the ground.

Men lined up on one side of the room and women on the other. If I could hum baroque music, they might just break into an Eighteenth Century dance, every movement prescribed. As though pacing off to a gavotte, the men began filling their plates; the older boys stood right behind them; the women and children waited their turns.

Elder Bonner, first in line, halted with a full plate, shouted out something about "giving thanks" and the line came to a grinding halt. "Bless this food; bless this fellowship; bless the hands that prepared it; bless it to our use." He halted for a moment, looked at the pile of choice white chicken pieces on his plate, and shouted: "Amen!"

I wandered over toward end of the line, not because I remembered my manners, but that's where Josh slouched against the far wall. Just as I was thinking about how to approach him, casually, so no one would notice; he shook his head very, very slowly as he narrowed his eyes.

Another set of eyes was making a beeline for me—Enoch Bonner with two over-flowing plates and an expression of joy on his moon-shaped face. The resemblance to Donnie Osmond, even a heavier Donnie, had disappeared.

Enoch, with his two plates of food, had the anticipatory air of a Greek, bearing gifts—no wooden horse in sight. He eased the plates onto a trestle table in front of me. "Got food for you already, Jenny. Your first time here at Wednesday Potluck. Pa says we can overlook the rules for once, and you can sit with me. He says it will be a courtesy to a newcomer."

I sat down backward on the bench and watched him struggling to get his big boots over the bench and under the table. "I hope you like fried chicken and them dumplings that Mama made. You can use a bit more flesh on you."

I leaned toward him in what I hoped was a provocative manner, planted my tennis shoes firmly in front of me for a quick getaway, and had just started to spew out the invective about "porky, lying weirdo" that was festering in my mouth when it happened again.

The lights went out. A small shriek went up, as though one of those sanctimonious hands had strayed under a table. The Saints were prepared. Candles and kerosene lanterns popped up along the tables as the men continued eating and the women created light.

Just about the time that most of the desserts were sinking into crumbs and frosting curls—before I'd had a bite of that gleaming chocolate cake that Maylene had made—Mr. Darken grabbed my arm.

A woman I recognized from the soap factory, one that Abigail had pointed out as Leah Winner, one of Elder Winner's wives, was with Mr. Darken, chattering like a magpie. "She knows her business. She really does, Mr. Darken. She whipped those things out of the fuse box, fixed them, and we've not had a bit of bother since. I told my husband about it, and he was that surprised."

"Elder Winner wants to talk to you, Jenny. He's responsible for general maintenance of our properties." Mr. Darken was hustling me across the room to a table where several older men picked over the bones of chicken and eyed me suspiciously. He pointed toward a tall, lean man with skin the color of raw bacon. The kerosene lamp cast odd shadows on people. A younger version of him sat beside him. He must be Jerry Winner, Abigail's "intended." She hovered nearby, refilling water glasses and giving me high-five signs with her eyes. I wasn't getting the message.

"I hear from my wife that you fixed the electrical problems in the canning building. She and Abigail . . ." He gestured with an idle flip of his hand toward the water bearer. "They said your pa trained you to be an electrician."

Not exactly, I wanted to shout. My father hoped I'd study mathematics in college. He taught me how things fit and how things work—clocks, fuses, electric currents, number theory, lengths, areas, volumes, and postulates. A straight line can be drawn from point to point, but not if the McKenzie River gets in the way.

This was no time for Euclid or modesty. I stood at attention and nodded soberly. I didn't want to make an affirmation so close to a church when it might come back to bite me. I could handle simple electrical projects—lamps, stoves, fuse boxes, plugs and—I was quite sure—the basic wiring on that electrical fence that kept us captive.

Elder Winner seemed to appreciate my self-conscious demeanor. "Girls don't usually do that kind of thing here—men's work. Though some of them drive the combine and tractors when harvest chores get to be too much. They're good help in a bind."

"We're in kind of a bind here now. Elder Grund— he's been the general factotum for anything to do with electricity here for a coon's age. They're keeping him in Spokane for a while to restent his heart. A kind of lube job if I get it right."

He hadn't, but no one dared to correct him. "They tell me it will be some time before he can get back to that kind of work. May not be able to do it at all if he gets one of them pacemakers. Won't be able to work with things that might shock him, though he's done a good job all these years at making things run."

Considering the plaits of cheap extension cord lining this room and the state of the fuse box in the soap factory, I wondered why this entire place hadn't gone up in smoke. I was giving some serious consideration to how I might make that happen, when Elder Winner made a sound like a loud fart. "Humph! We just have to hope the word doesn't get out that your girl's doing a man's work." He and Mr. Darken chuckled companionably while the other men at the table shot me dark looks. At least they looked very dark under the flicker of a kerosene flame.

"You can start in the morning on what's gone wrong with the electricity in the Community Room. The Lord's house comes first. Then, you can start checking the fence." Mr. Darken's frown punctuated the dim light, as though he knew I was getting the better of him without even trying.

"I know, Gomer. It's a two-edged sword. But, you know better than any man that we can't have our bulls getting out again. This entire compound depends on a good, strong current," he nodded deferentially toward the head of the table. "Elder Bonner says I can pull Josh Barnes off the computer now that the 990 return is almost done. He'll finish up the work."

I felt the compulsion to stare at Elder Bonner's eyes to see if little cherries or bells were rotating like a slot machine. If Josh's father had been prepared to notify the IRS, something was rotten in this ward of CPRC; now, Josh was being taken off-line.

"I figure that your girl can work faster with Josh driving the fence and helping with the equipment. The trickiest place will be getting down into them canyons to the west. Josh can haul a trailer with horses so they can get to those places where the truck can't go."

I ducked my head modestly as Mr. Darken mumbled something about supervision. The light in my eyes would have overshadowed a cluster of candles. I was going to be set free to roam about this place with Josh Barnes—free with the tools I needed to figure out how to drive the voltage around a circuit with resisters, capacitors, transformers, and switches that would bend to my will and send shock waves through the Compound.

Only a few things caused me concern. Josh Barnes was an unknown who made my pulse pound—first when he rescued me from Enoch, and, again, when I heard him playing Bach in the Zion Chapel. I wanted to think that we had a kind of connection, that he was not only warning me tonight about Enoch but about something even more threatening as he shook his head as slowly and precisely as a pendulum.

He obviously didn't like Enoch Bonner or Gomer Darken. But that didn't mean he wasn't tied body and soul to CPRC. People of this weird religious persuasion lived in Ptolemy's universe; the sun rotated around their world. Josh might or might not know that Elder Bonner had it in for his father—and, probably, for him. And. The most worrisome thing. I had never in my life been on a horse. The thought of sitting on a huge beast with yellow teeth terrified me.

"Can I borrow my friend?" Abigail wedged in between Mr. Darken and me. "She hasn't had a bite to eat. If she's going to deal with dangerous electrical wires, she needs to keep up her strength."

Abigail was not only a water bearer but an eavesdropper. She steered me to the far end of the food table. "Couldn't you see me sending you signals? I wanted you to see Zeb. I wouldn't dare introduce you. I'm already in big trouble, because my pa saw me touch his hand when I was filling water glasses. I'll get a hiding when I get home, but it was worth it. Zeb's that good-looking boy that was standing over there by Josh."

I turned toward the wall where Josh had been. Abigail spun me back toward her as though I might reveal a secret. "He's not there now. He and Josh left a few minutes ago, after my pa had words with him. Zeb and Josh were good friends as kids. They both live in the SYM house, but Zeb says Josh has become a loner since his pa died."

Abigail pulled me down and fished around on a near-empty platter for a chicken wing. "They've picked everything clean. I was just using it as an excuse to get you away from the elders—so we could talk away from work where all the women can hear us. We're friends, aren't we?" Her hazel eyes had such a hopeful expression that I gave her a quick hug.

"That means what we say stays with each of us. That's not the way it is with our people. There are not supposed to be any secrets—not from the Elders or our parents. They say being open and honest keeps us pure in the eyes of God. That means we can't keep things that we might want to." Her eyes flushed with tears.

"I never had a friend like you, a girl who knows about important things. Zeb says he and Josh used to talk about everything . . . until his father had that accident. Then Josh clammed up, told Zeb he couldn't trust anyone." Abigail looked as though she had just lost her best friend.

I squeezed her fingers and felt a little disgusted with myself for milking the cow again. "Why can't he trust anyone, especially his friend? What could Zeb have to do with his father's death?"

"Simon MacAfee, that's Zeb's pa, manages the dairy herd. That bull tried to gore him once, but he was too quick for it. He wanted to get rid of it, said he was afraid for the children to be around such an animal. Elder Bonner wouldn't go for it. It makes good calves. Something about the bloodline. That's what Zeb told me. He said his pa probably wasn't anywhere near the barn, but he wasn't sure. Mr. MacAfee got there when Josh found his pa all bloody and messy. Josh had already stuck a pitchfork in that bull right on the spot." The shock in Abigail's eyes wasn't reflected in mine. Served the bull right in my opinion.

"Elder Bonner sent Josh to SYM to live with the older boys. Said his mother should have raised him not to harm a high-priced bull. He said no one was responsible for the carelessness of Josh's father." Abigail rubbed her hands as though she might be imitating Pontius Pilate absolving himself of a crime.

She was guilty as sin of something. At least, the expression on her father's face made that clear to both of us. "Abigail, you are supposed to be helping clean up in the kitchen not jawing with the new girl. The Winners are ready to leave. You need to say goodnight to Jeremiah and his family. They'll be yours before long. Then, you won't need to make other acquaintances."

The bleak, shameful expression on Abigail's face haunted me as she followed her father, her sack-like dress clinging to a body that was quite shapely. Would he really give her a "hiding" for simply touching the hand of Zeb? If Marybeth would switch a seven-year-old child for letting a cat in the house, Abigail's father might not hesitate to use a cat of nine tails on his daughter.

That was the real crime here. Who cared if they stockpiled weapons to fight off an invasion of non-believers? Who cared if they gypped the IRS out of tax money? Lots of multi-millionaires did that as routine business practice. The real crime was trafficking in women.

The CPRCers wouldn't see it that way. Males at the top of the Great Chain of Being, right under the angels. What was it that Mr. Darken said when I revealed him as a two-timing bigamist? "Men *are* that they might have joy."

The men in this Compound, that self-righteous bunch of so-called elders and apostles, *used* women the same way that women in some Muslim cultures allow. No long black burkas to cover everything but their eyeballs, but the saggy, floral fifties house dresses made even less of a fashion statement. The cheap polyester fabric accented fat thighs, generous rumps, and hid cleavage.

CHAPTER 14

Showing cleavage could get a girl in trouble around here, as Marybeth proclaimed over gelatinous oatmeal the next morning.

Lorena put both hands over her bowl, refusing the glob hanging from a serving ladle. "Why can't we ever have Captain Crunch or Lucky Charms?"

Marybeth ignored her. "A spoke-for girl like Abigail Johnson shouldn't leave her blouse open to her navel while she prances around serving water, leaning over men folks. Causes her family no end of worry."

I glanced up at Marybeth whose thick neck descended like a pillar into a sea of rendered lard. Exposure wasn't a risk she'd be taking. Best to keep silent. I learned more when I let Marybeth natter on without the benefit of my cryptic comments.

It was a "girls' morning" around the breakfast table after the Potluck. Maylene informed us that Mr. Darken had left early for a Council Meeting in Coeur d'Alene, a regular monthly meeting for some of the men. I'd mark that on my mental calendar. It would be best to make our escape when the Elders and Apostles were away.

"Abigail has always been such an obliging girl, a pearl of a girl, I always said when she was in my classroom. Never caused bother. Except now to her father." Maylene smiled benignly as though her words might end up carved in stone.

Maylene's quirky turn of phrases annoyed me. Now, she was into a rhyming mode, probably imagining herself as some kind of vagabond poet like Whitman or Verlaine. I didn't know whether to gag over the verse or the oatmeal.

"Abigail will be heading to the altar sooner than planned. Miz Johnson told me so herself last night at the Potluck. Things was settled by Elder Winner and Mr. Johnson six months ago, but Zeb MacAfee's been a trial to the Johnson family taking notice of Abigail like he does."

"Is that the pretty little redhead you introduced me to last night, Jenny?" Compound gossip usually made Mother's eyes glaze over, as though she'd tuned into a soap opera she wouldn't be watching for long. "She can't be much older than you. Surely a girl that young can't be thinking of marriage."

"She isn't. Her father is thinking for her. She's six months older than me, fifteen last August. She told me that her intended, Jerry Winner, is twenty. Under federal law, he should go to jail. Even if she wanted to marry him and her parents consented, she has to be at least sixteen." I wanted to add that she absolutely did not want to marry Jerry Winner, but I dared not share Abigail's secret.

"The wedding won't take place for a year. She may change her mind before then." Mother settled things nicely for Abigail. No fuss. No bother. Just a change of mind.

"She won't. She can't. She is betrothed to Jerry Winner. Zeb MacAfee has been sent to live in the ward down by Boise, so he won't be troubling her no more. The ceremony is set for next Saturday. I will let her go back to the sewing room so she can whip herself up something nice for her wedding. She's right good on the sewing machine." Marybeth could settle someone's future faster than a hydrogen bomb.

"I expect you can make one of your big white layer cakes, Maylene? I'm sure Miz Johnson would appreciate the gesture." Marybeth set the oatmeal pot down with a thump on the stove. "Get those electric tools, Jenny. I'll walk you over to the chapel. You need to fix whatever went wrong."

WHATEVER WENT WRONG started some time Thursday morning. A general alarm had gone up at noon when Abigail didn't come home for lunch from the sewing room where she'd been "allowed" to go to sew up her own wedding dress.

I had spent most of the day working out the intricacies of the mess of wiring in the Community Room. Mice had nibbled away the thermoplastic insulation on many of the wires. Elder Grund could count himself lucky that his heart was on the mend in Spokane.

Someone who had a penchant for cutting off the third prong of plugs and overloading an outlet with them was flirting with a serious shock.

"You! Jenny Hatchet. Do you know where my girl has gone? Where she might be hiding? What she might be up to?" Abigail Johnson's mother came barreling toward me as she burst into the Community Room. Her rusty orange hair stood up in spikes, like little antennas set on finding a missing daughter.

She was in need of calming before she ended up in the hospital with Elder Grund. I led her over to a chair and poured her a glass of water. "I haven't seen Abigail since the Potluck last night. I've been here all day working. Marybeth told me that Abigail had been reassigned to the sewing room to work on her . . . dress." I couldn't choke out the word "wedding."

"I give her a good breakfast this morning, trying to patch things up because of her pa." Her woebegone expression suggested that the patching wasn't helpful. "She's never been a headstrong girl. Always let us decide what's best for her. Her pa might have been overly forceful last night."

I tried for a compassionate face, but I knew I was looking at her from disbelieving eyes. "Overly forceful" probably meant Mr. Johnson had whipped the holy shit out of his daughter. Her mother's solution to injury of body and spirit was a "good breakfast."

"She *was* supposed to go to the sewing room this morning after she seen Jerry Winner, but she never showed up at his folks' place or the sewing room. She told me she was going to see Jerry to 'settle things' before she went to work on her dress. She shot out of the house without eating a bite. She planned on helping me get some rose cuttings in this afternoon," Mrs. Johnson added hopefully, as though Abigail might be just outside with her shears.

"He ain't seen her. Miz Winner and Jerry was having their noon meal. Elder Winner went with the other men to the Council Meeting. I looked in all her old hidey places in the barn, down by the creek where she liked to catch tadpoles when she was young." Her shoulders slumped. "I don't know why she'd worry me like this."

I did, but I had enough concern about Abigail— mainly that she might have found a way to run off with Zeb MacAfee—to join the search. It was mostly women and children pacing off the grounds and calling her name. The older boys were working in the fields. A troublesome girl who had only been missing a few hours would show up by sunset.

When the sun was casting long, low streamers through the bank of Douglas firs at the far end of the heifer pasture, something did show up. Abigail's shoe. I saw it lying by a path that the cattle had made to the feeder just this side of the fence. Just one small shoe, oddly scraped on one side. No mate.

Maylene made a call from Mr. Darken's office to his cell phone. "Emergencies only," she muttered. No rhyming this time. The men had already left the meeting in Coeur d'Alene and were on their way home. Within minutes, the phone in his office rang. Maylene stood in the door of his office and said quietly. "Gomer called the other ward. Zeb MacAfee is there. He hasn't seen Abigail since Wednesday."

Two of Moses Blair's half-breed beagles sniffed the shoe, and the hunt started again. I pointed to the exact spot next to the cow path where I'd spotted the shoe— simply because I'd had the presence of mind to mark the corner fence post with my pocket knife. All the prints along the muddy path seemed to confuse the dogs. They sniffed the shoe and trotted off, then back, then off again. Aimlessly, it seemed to me. The ability to scent must have been bred out of them.

Led by Jerry and Enoch, the older boys arced beams from flashlights through the forest of firs and pines as they followed old logging roads into the woods.

Finally, the children were sent home; the women and older girls set up food on the backs of pickups as though they were at a tailgate party; no one was having fun. By midnight, an exhausted crew prepared to go home and leave the Johnsons to their grief.

After leading the fruitless charge into the forest, Jerry Winner looked as though he might be having a bad day, but his sulky, put-upon expression struck me as almost furtive.

"First light, we'll go at it again. We'll find our girl." As he laid an arm companionably across Mr. Johnson's shoulders, Elder Winner not only took charge of the hunt; he was claiming ownership of the missing Abigail.

I watched Abigail's mother standing on the mound of freshly mulched soil in her rose bed, turning to stone like Niobe on Mount Sipylus. While her flinty face could still move, she shouted after a disappearing Elder Winner and his son: "Something ain't right here! Something's gone terribly wrong!"

CHAPTER 15

Whatever went wrong could never be fixed by any living creature. When they fished Abigail out of the stock pond near the heifer pasture on Friday afternoon, the pockets of her long coat were packed with stones.

A muddy stock pond lacks the élan of the River Ouse for last rites like those for Virginia Woolf, but we could hear shouts so full of grief that neither obscurity nor celebrity made a whit of difference in the sense of loss. The four boys carrying Abigail back to the porch of her house had been her childhood playmates. I could not bear to watch and wandered off to be by myself.

THAT EVENING, MOTHER, Mr. Darken, Lorena, and I made a silent quartet around the kitchen table. Mr. Darken picked at a brazen haunch of ham. Marybeth had gone upstairs in a huff when Maylene, returning from the Johnson house mid-afternoon with red-rimmed and watery eyes, ignored her questions about the state of the family and the body.

When a light tapping sounded at the front door, Mr. Darken pushed back his chair, grumbling about who-in-the-world-at-this-time-of-night. He came back into the kitchen with a puzzled expression. "Mrs. Johnson, Abigail's mother, wants to see you, Jenny. She wants you to go to the chapel with her. She said you were Abigail's best friend." He seemed ready to make another comment, but Mother's expression would not allow a word.

"Would you like to see Abigail, Jenny? She's fixed up nice. Maylene did the bathing and put real flowers in her hair. I don't know where she got them this time of year. The funeral is tomorrow, but all the people will be there. They'll come from other wards, beings she's so young and her betrothal and all." Tears streamed down Mrs. Johnson's face as though the thought of a ceremony around her daughter's death was too much to bear.

I had never seen a dead body in my life. My father's casket was closed so that I could only imagine what pieces of him were fished from the McKenzie River. I wanted to decline the invitation, to tell Abigail's mother that "her betrothal and all" might have pushed her daughter over the edge.

Instead, I put my arm around the sobbing woman and wept with her all the way to Zion Chapel.

The lights were low, lights that I had restored the day Abigail went missing. We walked to a bier with a plain wooden casket on it. The face in the box had "gone off," become something other than what it was supposed to be, like the sour milk that Marybeth mixed with the fresh, hoping we wouldn't notice.

Mrs. Johnson stroked the side of Abigail's frozen face. "She was so pretty. She was the prettiest baby in the church nursery. All the other mothers were that jealous. Maylene thought she should wear a choir robe. She so loved the singing." She tweaked a small strand of bright hair that had managed to curl in spite of the straightening that had been inflicted on it.

"Elder Winner is an important man here. Jerry is his oldest son. He will come into his pa's property and rights. That gains him a larger share. Abigail's pa wanted her to have the security that we never had. Some of us bring only hard work. Most of the old families have ownership. That's what *he* wanted for her." There was an angry emphasis on "he."

I had the sense that the woman trailing her fingers alongside the face of this dead girl was in the process of distancing herself from her husband. "Maylene seen the marks on her body. She didn't say a thing though. He only ever hit her on her backside. He never ever hit her legs. She must have got those scratches on the front of her legs somewheres else. The top of her bare foot was scraped something pitiful. Maylene took special care not to hurt it."

Never before had I noticed the kind of delicately squared off line of Abigail's jaw. She might have been Garbo as Camille, a beautiful creature who would always be dying but never really dead because she longed for more than she was given.

A line from a poem that our English teacher had read to us by Louise Gluck kept running through my head: ". . . to be one thing is next to nothing."

That's what these people wanted Abigail to become—a sisterwife. And that's why she tried to run, why she lost a shoe trying to run, and why she finally gave up and chose to walk with rocks into the water.

The bright eyes of Abigail lay beneath lids that were already hollowing into lifelessness. Her pale lips would never again make a joke about Jerry Winner. At that moment, it struck me: *de omnibus dubitantum.* Doubt everything. I did remember some Latin. I needed to share Descartes' advice to be suspicious of everything with Josh.

No one would walk shoeless through that cow pasture with hacked off stubs of brush poking up along the fence line where the cow path wound. Scratches on the front of her legs and the top of her bare foot might mean she had been dragged along the path.

I did something then that I would never, ever believe myself capable of doing. I leaned over Abigail as though I might be planting a last sad kiss on her forehead, gently pulled the collar of the prim robe aside, and stared at a neck bearing a pattern of discolorations that all the talcum powder in the world couldn't hide.

ABIGAIL'S MOTHER WAS right. The CPRCers turned out in droves for the funeral. Cars and trucks with people I'd never seen lined the gravel road clear down to the big gates, unlocked for the occasion.

Like a bereaved widower, Jerry Winner sat between his mother and Elder Winner, with the three additional

Winner wives stacked up like pale pancakes to make room in the front pew for Abigail's parents.

As the Darken harem, as I thought of us now, entered the chapel, I could see Enoch Bonner in the pew behind the grieving families, motioning like a spastic windmill in our direction.

"Enoch's saved a place for you, Jenny. Place of honor, behind your friend's family. You go on. We'll sit at the back." Between the pressure of Mr. Darken's hand against my spine and the possibility of being beheaded by Enoch's ulna, I made the only choice possible: escape.

I eased along the back wall until I came to that small recessed alcove with the old cucking stool. It seemed fitting to squat down on an ancient stool meant for disobedient women. Elder Bonner took the podium and tried not to scold Abigail for taking her life. "Not in her right mind," he assured her grieving parents. "Your child has gone to God."

That gave me the only comfort I'd felt for two days. The choir, wearing robes that matched Abigail's, sang of "a sunny land whose skies are ever bright . . . where joy can never die." I hoped a happier Abigail was in a sunny place. Outside, dark clouds gathered and rain began falling, listlessly, as though it didn't really care if it fell.

Like a primitive ritual, the speechless assembly filed by the open casket for a last look at Abigail. Then, Elder Bonner snapped the lid closed and announced: "The funeral meal is being set up in the Community Room as we speak. Because of the weather, we'll honor the wishes of the Johnsons to have only a few of us at the interment."

With the precision of a military escort, a quartet of boys who had outgrown their Sunday suits lifted the casket effortlessly and marched down the aisle.

I shrunk down on the stool, pressing my back into the corner, closing my eyes, trying to be invisible so that I wouldn't feel the weight of guilt that came with every breath that Abigail could no longer take.

Sharp fingers pressed into my shoulder. Enoch had found me. No. He wouldn't dare stroke my frozen face as though it might be the last human touch I'd feel.

"Jenny. I'd like for you to come with me to see Abigail put to rest. If you think you can bear it." The doleful face of Mrs. Johnson peered down at me. Her husband stood behind her with a half-raised hand—as though he either wanted to strike her, or elevate me. I stood on my own, let her take my hand, refused an umbrella and walked out into a cleansing rain holding the arm of a dry-eyed woman.

Great swooping branches of Douglas fir shook silver drops into a raw trench that troubled their roots. Abigail's roots were all around her, modest gray stones propped up over Johnsons: "Blessed are the pure in heart," "The righteous shall go to life eternal," and, "Blessed are they that mourn for they shall be comforted."

The sense of hopefulness graven into the old stones lifted my spirits a bit. I was almost assured that Abigail might be singing with the angels, almost, but not quite.

CHAPTER 16

The thundercloud of Marybeth's face loomed over me the next morning as I prissily buttered triangles of toast and turned a blind eye to the oatmeal she shoved in front of me. "I don't approve of a single girl, particularly one as bull-headed as you are, gallivanting around the country with Josh Barnes."

She splashed some of her sour milk mixture on the oatmeal. "It's just not done, especially with you being too friendly with that poor, dead girl. Made a right show at the funeral with Miz Johnson. I had words with Mr. Darken about it. They'll be questions. Not seemly."

Not seemly that an innocent girl died? They'll be questions about her death? Abigail's mother and I offended the funeral crowd? Trying to sort out Marybeth's grudges could get my day off to a bad start.

The 1980s Chevy pickup with a horse trailer behind it sat idling in the front yard. I didn't expect a knock on the door. With Marybeth eyeing me suspiciously and glaring out the window at Josh, I needed to make this little venture all about the business of being an electrician—not about a fifteen-year-old girl who had stolen her bigamist stepfather's razor to shave her legs and swiped her mother's lace boy-cut underwear just in case. In case of what, I really hadn't figured out. They were clean if we had a car wreck.

Mother had packed a lunch for us before heading off for her tutorial on the CPRC gospel on how not to kill yeast if you wanted bread to rise.

I grabbed my tool pouch and stepped outside with what I hoped was a confident swagger. Josh was leaning against the passenger's door. He grabbed my bag and flung it into the back, and walked around to open his own door.

"Your stepmother is eyeing us," he said.

"Yeah. She thinks we plan to fornicate up and down the length of the south pasture." I thought I'd give him a wake-up call first thing this morning, not let him think that I was one of those simpering girls watching him piously from church pews.

He didn't even lift an eyebrow. Instead, he pulled out an iPod that looked well used, fiddled with something on what might have once been a radio, and shoved a plug in the space where a cigarette lighter once lived.

"Do you ever get the feeling that you're missing the mark . . . it's so cold . . . so cold." Coldplay soared out of the dashboard of that old pickup. I felt as though I had just left Mars and landed squarely back on Mother Earth.

"Where in the world did you . . ." I was lost for words. The Bach surprised me. Coldplay amazed me.

"This was my father's pickup. We wired it for my iPod. I listen when I'm working away from the others—used to listen at my house, until I got moved to SYM. It will be our guilty secret," he smiled an absolutely devilish Jude Law grin that caused my backbone to collapse like a train of dominos. Real music. Real sound. Something besides Maylene's dreadful versifying and Marybeth's proselytizing.

My defenses were down. If he happened to have "Every Teardrop Is a Waterfall" on his iPod, I'd be lost. Total surrender. I sat upright. Control is essential. Josh Barnes might provide a way to get my mother, Lorena and me out of this prison. Or he might not. Wheels did not make for a clean escape with electric fences circling the Compound and faster cars than old pickups in sheds.

"Stop here, by that first corner post. I need to check the insulators—be sure that the ground port and fence ports check out." Elder Winner had given me access to the tool shed where the ailing Elder Grund kept his supplies. The voltmeter with a metal ground probe would come in handy for checking the charge along the fence. While I was in the shed, I nabbed a six-inch, fixed-blade knife, a roll of paracord, and a small, collapsible shovel.

A canvas tote covered with mouse pellets and spider webs had been pushed to the back of a shelf. I shook it out, crammed things in it, and hurried out of the shed. With a plastic tarp, matches, and food, I'd have a survival kit if I needed it.

I walked the fence to the furthest point from the battery energizer, stuck the voltmeter into the ground beneath the fence, and touched the red clip to the wire. The charge was OK.

The truck pulling alongside of us was not. Enoch Bonner beamed from behind the wheel. "I'm here to help you, Jenny."

"Thought you and Jerry were supposed to be moving the heifers onto the spring wheat this morning, Enoch." Josh's voice was measured and low.

"Told Pa I'd rather help Jenny check the fence. You go work cattle. It would be easier to switch trucks so we don't have to unload the horses and hook the trailer to my truck," Enoch royally sorted out the morning chores as though he were born to the throne.

Josh swung the heavy tote up, dropped it into the back of the pickup, and opened the passenger side of the truck in one fluid movement. "Ready to move on, Jenny? You said you wanted to get to the posts in the canyon first."

I had said no such thing. Getting into the canyon meant getting onto the back of one of those ill-tempered horses kicking the sides of the trailer. Anything was better than getting into a pickup with Enoch Bonner.

I could feel his sour breath against the side of my face. The over-sized biceps stretching his too-tight plaid shirt suggested a dependence on steroids; that might explain the moon face—Cushing's syndrome.

Nope. Not Cushing's. Not with that testosterone rush behind the hand crushing my arm. Instinctively, I whopped my elbow against Enoch's solar plexus without even considering his liver or gall bladder.

A wave of nausea hit me about the same time it hit Enoch. I might have permanently damaged Elder Bonner's son. Bent double, Enoch couldn't seem to suck in enough wind.

Josh just stood there looking pleased as Enoch smacked aside his helping hand. "I expect Jenny doesn't like work schedules being changed so arbitrarily. You'd best be getting to the wheat pasture."

As I eased past Enoch and climbed into the passenger's seat, Josh hopped in, cranked up Coldplay, and steered the pickup along a double grassy track that led up and up along a fence that meandered beside us—and then dropped into a void.

"Good move, Jenny. You could teach the girls around here something about discouraging suitors." Josh was easing the truck onto a small level patch of grass dangerously near the edge of a gorge.

"Suitor? That . . . that . . . churl." It was the most ladylike thing I could call the oaf that had just caused considerable pain to shoot up my humerus from contact with his ribs. "You have to be kidding. No one in their right mind would . . ."

"You think your stepfather is in his right mind? Or Elder Bonner? Or Elder Winner? I don't think you understand how the minds of men who sit on the Ward Council work. My mother does. That's why . . ." He stopped abruptly, as though he had said too much, pocketed his iPod, and swung down from his truck.

The trailer gate screeched open as Josh backed out a fat gray mare and an over-sized bay. He tightened the cinches on their saddles and looped the reins through the trailer vents.

I froze. The trail into the canyon was absolutely perpendicular, ninety degrees, no give or take. I envisioned those old cowboy movies in which herds of horses raced up to the edge and plunged down, their forelegs scooping up dirt like front loaders.

"Why don't you show me how to use that tester thing in your bag? You don't have to do this. I'll loan you my iPod. If Enoch shows up with Jerry Winner, just lock the pickup doors and honk."

I wasn't about to school anyone in the Compound about the ins and outs of electricity. My so-called capabilities were what got me out of the soap factory today, out into the wilds with Josh, and what might get me through the fence with my mother and sister.

"Too dangerous. Not something a novice should be doing," I said with an arch smile. "I'm not fond of horses, so I'll just walk down the trail."

"I don't think so. Not wearing those," he pointed toward my tennis shoes. "Western Rattlesnakes don't usually come up this far, and it's still early in the year; you never know though. You should have worn boots." He pointed to my skirt. "And long pants under that thing."

The voluminous skirt with its elastic band hung mid-calf, an out-of-fashion hemline—never mind the puce tulips galloping above my knees. Terror gave way to humiliation. I hiked it up and stalked over to the bay horse.

"Not the gelding. He's jumpy. I brought Sally for you. She's an old ladies' horse. Perfectly safe. I'll hold her while you mount. I might need to adjust your stirrups."

And insult me left and right in my "old lady" flowery skirt. Safe horse. I'd show him safe. I hoisted up my right foot. Wrong foot. Shifted. Stuck my left foot up and felt very strong hands circling my waist and lifting me as though I had become weightless.

Like a sail in high wind, my skirt billowed out and up until there was no doubt in my mind that Josh Barnes would have any trouble describing my mother's pink lace panties to the other boys in SYM.

Riding a wild horse down the side of a canyon is a piece of cake. You simply keep your eyes closed, your head ducked so branches don't swat you off, and cling to the saddle horn as though it's the only friend you'll ever have. When I opened my eyes again, the horses were grazing on a grassy area next to a small stream. Josh had dismounted, put my tote on the ground, and was spreading a blanket.

I fastened my eyes on the metal fence posts, studying the insulators clipped around them as though they were the most fascinating objects I'd ever seen. I knew that old-style cowboys traveled with a blanket on the back of their saddles. Bringing a blanket on a first date in the land of the Saints was a bit outré.

It really wasn't a date. I leaned forward on Sally, swung my right leg over her back, crushed my knees together and slid down. The blessed horse didn't move, just kept gnawing away at grass stubble. I picked up my bag and stalked off toward the first t-post.

"Leave it, Jenny. You're the only one who knows how many problems, if any, this fence might have. Don't be in a hurry. You can make this job last for a long time if you're clever. I know you're clever, but popping Enoch a good one probably wasn't the best idea you've had."

He lifted one eyebrow in the face of my self-righteous grunt. "Don't get me wrong. I did enjoy it. I've been thinking about repercussions. Enoch's been spreading rumors that his father and Mr. Darken are about to come to an agreement."

I dropped like a rock to the blanket, pulled my knees up to my chin, and stared up at Josh. "An agreement." I was afraid to ask the question. I didn't want an answer.

"Enoch acts like a bully when he has an audience, but he's too stupid to do much harm. It's his buddy, Jerry Winner, who concerns me. I'm not sure you've met him."

"No, and I don't want to meet him. I blame him for what happened to Abigail." I shot Josh a fierce, introspective glance. "There might be things that you . . ."

"That I don't know? You might be amazed at what I know or think I know, Jenny." He looked pensively toward the grazing horses. "It's best to let Abigail lie in her grave. For now. She's past being hurt. It's Jerry that poses a threat. He's got a screw loose. Plays Enoch like a fiddle. And gets exactly what he wants. That might be you."

Suddenly within me I felt that the thread holding my arms and legs onto my body had snapped. Like a well-used puppet, I felt older, as though fifteen was just a number and had nothing to do with the experience of life.

The hand that stroked my hair was soft. I closed my eyes, wrapped my arms around my legs and tried to retreat as far away as I could. Rustling noises intruded. Maybe the dreaded Western Rattlesnake. Or, a small feast spread out on the blanket. Not the slabs of rat cheese on plain bread that Mother had packed.

Pale deviled eggs with a splash of paprika circled one plate. Creamy potato salad mounded next to bright green tabouli. Small fingerlings of fresh bread were coated with cream cheese and thin slices of cucumber.

"Your mother told Mom that you prefer vegetarian dishes, and that living on Marybeth's cooking is giving all of you a grease overload. She thought you might like a change. Not exactly a workman's lunch. Hope you like it."

"I love it! I haven't seen tabouli since Portland. Where did your mother find fresh parsley out here in the hinterlands?"

"Her greenhouse. The flowers for Abigail's funeral came from there. She keeps it warm in the winter with a wood stove. Lots of work. The Council won't approve any other kind of heat though she shares vegetables with their families." Josh picked up a cucumber sandwich. "Perfect rectangles. Your mother told Mom that you read Euclid for fun."

"Used to. Mr. Darken's library consists of the *Book of Mormon* and out-of-date *Farmers' Almanacs*. My brain is turning to mush, like Marybeth's puddings and vats of lye soap."

"I'll sneak you some books out of our library. Mother won't mind."

"You have a library? Real books? Not just Bibles?" I thought the closest library might be in Bonners' Ferry, but I had little chance of ever getting into it. I had even less chance of retrieving my MacBook and getting online. A page of print that had nothing to do with righteousness or the weather would tickle me into spasms.

By mid-afternoon, the sun was dropping into the firs, and we had talked ourselves hoarse. I learned that Josh's father was a certified CPA, that he met Josh's mother at Brigham Young University, and that they had returned to the CPRC fold before Josh was born because of his grandparents' health problems. He said that just before his father died, they had discussed leaving.

"But, Mother was raised here. This life was all she knew before her parents sent her to BYU. My grandparents were born here. And theirs. Many of the families go back over a hundred years. The lichen covers up the dates and names on those stones, but we have a long history here."

I shot him a skeptical look, wondering how many generations had endured the madness of this place.

"It wasn't always like it is now. Most of the first families were normal—monogamous farming families. Some of those who moved in later got booted out of Salt Lake City for believing they were reincarnations of Abraham, Jacob, David, and Solomon."

My blank look seemed to irritate him. "Polygamists, Jenny. Old Testament. You really should study the Bible. St. James' version, if you like, but it is part of history. Most of the families in this Ward have monogamous marriages."

He frowned into the low-hanging sun. "The big land owners here, Elder Bonner, Elder Winner, and Mr. Darken, are reversing that trend as fast as they can. How in the world did your mother get hooked up with Mr. Darken?"

"Lies. Duplicity. A two-carat diamond. A pledge to look after her children. A whirlwind secret court-ship with the promise that the Garden of Eden had been discovered in Northern Idaho. No mention of two more wives at home." I couldn't keep the anger out of my voice. "Poisonous snakes. Pedophiles. Killers of girls. That's his Eden."

"I'd be very careful about what I say aloud around here. There are lots of ears, none very friendly to strangers." Josh began rolling up the blanket and tossing the leftovers to a noisy Stellar's jay, hopping from limb to limb, flouting his Elvis Presley 50s crest.

"It's not what I say. It's what I hear and what I see. For instance . . ." I rolled out the phrase to get Josh's full attention. He seemed more interested in the birds than what I had to say. "Just this past week, I overheard Mr. Darken and Elder Bonner discussing you and your father. They said you might know too much for your own good."

I tried to plaster on a sympathetic smile as he turned a rigid face to me. "Something about sticking a pitchfork in a murdering bull." I touched his arm. "I do admire revenge, Josh. It shows spirit."

What a lame comment to make to someone who found his father gored and trampled past imagining— and then slaughtered a bull that was just doing what mad bulls do. I amended it with information that might get his attention. "I want revenge for Abigail—against whoever strangled her and dumped her in the pond."

"That's exactly what I mean, Jenny. You open your mouth, and very careless words come out that could do great harm to you and your family."

Well, shut my mouth. Pouting, I walked over to the point of the far post where a makeshift cover of an energizer hung at an angle. Corroded terminals, tree limbs on the fence, dead batteries—I could extend my fence project for weeks and no one would be the wiser. The section next to the main gate could wait until I was ready to hightail it out of this harem.

I disconnected the battery terminals, picked up the energizer and dropped it in my tote. Then I swung my bag along with my very awkward body onto Sally's back.

"Saddle up, Tonto. Or should I say Watson? He never could get the drift of anything either."

Apologizing might be an easy out for some. Josh's silence on the drive back invited me to eat humble pie. I've never liked the taste of humility. Especially when I am right.

It had taken more courage than I thought I had to bend low over Abigail to sneak a peek at her neck so that her mother wouldn't see what I was doing. She probably thought I was kissing that stone-cold face. The marks were there. Irregular patches as though big hands had gripped Abigail's thin neck. I had expected Josh to ask why I thought she'd been strangled, to commend me for my discovery. He should want retribution for Abigail. Instead, he had criticized me for making imprudent comments.

When the pickup rattled into the front yard, a hellhound guarded the premises. Mr. Darken cocked his head toward me, then toward Josh, and then behind him—just like a three-headed Cerberus on patrol.

"I thought you were going to be up by the heifer pasture. That's where the fence quit working. Enoch told me you'd gone down into the far canyon. That wasn't the plan. You should know better, Josh. I've a mind to take a strap to you."

"Not the best idea, Mr. Darken."

With a snarl that could frighten a mythological beast, Mr. Darken stepped back to the safety of the porch and shouted: "Off my property, now! You won't be driving out with Jenny any longer. I've seen to that. Elder Winner agrees. He's assigned his boy to help."

An image of Jerry Winner—hunkered over with what he thought might pass for grief as four boys carried her coffin out of the church—flashed before me.

"I'm not going anywhere with Jerry Winner. I'd rather be boiled in oil, drawn and quartered, dismembered . . ."

"I'd entertain that possibility before I'd let you get into a vehicle with Josh Barnes again." Mr. Darken interrupted. "Now get yourself into the house. Your mother is worried."

She wasn't. She was sitting very quietly by the window watching Mr. Darken waving his fist at a retreating pickup. "I like the looks of Josh, Jenny. His mother says such nice things about her son. We talk, you know, when I have my sessions with her. She's a potter. Has a kiln. Does a fair bit of business with her wares. She thinks I have a knack."

Mother had a knack for keeping quiet at the right time. I must have missed that gene. The slam of the front door reverberated through the house as Mr. Darken turned his contorted face toward me. "You just wait until tomorrow morning, young lady. You just wait."

I would wait until the "dawn came up like thunder outer China cross the bay" before I got into a pickup with Jerry Winner. I was the only electrician wanna-be that stood between a fence and lot of cows that might like trekking right up into Canada. I intended to let that be my argument.

CHAPTER 17

If I could sandwich in a run before breakfast, it was allowed. I needed to run until my arches ached from wearing tennis shoes not designed for running—and my lungs almost burst with great drafts of pure mountain air.

I stepped out onto the front porch into a glorious morning and screamed. A little circlet of quail rested inches from the door. With their bloody heads, eyes filmed over, and lifeless wings touching, it appeared as though someone had created a macabre Christmas wreath out of bird bodies.

"If I didn't know better, I'd say you've got an admirer." Marybeth swooped up the dead quail as though she might be the recipient.

Maybe gifting dead birds was some kind of primitive dating ritual. Other primitive rituals such as *droit du seigneur*, the right of the lord of the manor to be the first to bed the bride on her wedding night, probably held sway around this godforsaken Compound.

"Tomorrow, we'll have quail with biscuits and *my* gravy. What a treat. Especially out of season."

Two more strikes against Enoch if he had slaughtered these birds. Marybeth's gravy could rivet the GI track more solidly than Rosie could nail a battleship—and hunting out of season was illegal. Probably not on CPRC land. The word legal didn't seem to be in their lexicon.

No sooner had Marybeth hauled off the corpses of the quail than a big red Ford truck pulled into the yard, smashing a row of Maylene's newly planted geraniums.

Hitler hopped out. From his polished brown knee-high boots, to the tiny smudge of a mustache above his upper lip, clear up to the slab of oily hair plastered low to hide a receding hairline, Jeremiah Winner might have just dropped in from the Third Reich.

The ice-blue eyes calculating my reaction left me no doubt.

"I don't think we've met formally, Jenny, but I know quite a bit about you. From Abigail." He lifted one boot, then the other, as though he might begin goose-stepping across the lawn, polishing the tops of them on the backs of his calves.

I doubted that. At the Potluck, Abigail was eager for me to see her friend Zeb MacAfee. As I recalled, she had next to nothing to say about her intended. For once, I was silent, staring him down as though he were an unwelcome intruder.

"Mr. Darken said you'd be helping Jenny with the fence today, Jerry. That's a relief to the family. Not someone like Josh." Marybeth looked askance at Maylene's squashed flowers. "No matter." She brightened. "I fixed a good lunch for you. Mr. Darken wants the south fence worked on first. You'll know where to take her."

The ovens. Dachau. Buchenwald. Ravensbrüch. That was the concentration camp for women. I was one up on Mr. Jeremiah Winner. With a good charger, an electric fence not properly grounded can deliver a powerful jolt. Considering the leaky old batteries, broken insulators and shredded wires I had seen, only the memory of a shock must be holding the cattle away.

I could refuse to go with Jerry or I could let him trail me along the fence and try to set traps for him. I stared at his big hands hanging uselessly by his side and wondered if his thumbs matched the splotches on Abigail's neck.

"This is my new truck, Jenny. Pa bought it for me to help me forget . . . that I was . . . you know. Feeling under the weather." After fumbling for the words to describe what he should be feeling, Jerry recovered with aplomb. "A pretty girl like you ought to be ashamed to be seen in that old heap of Josh's. I'll show you what a 4-valve V-8 will do. Take our minds off things."

At that moment, I knew I was not facing a villain like Sherlock's Professor Moriarty who had "a brain of the first order." Jerry's brain might easily be mistaken for Marybeth's pudding.

I walked the south fence finding low voltmeter readings in several places. Jerry trailed behind me like an irritating wasp. With power below 3,000 volts, the cattle could get out. With power below 4,000 volts the wildlife would breach the fence. I knew the answer before I got past the main corner post and saw that the energizer was inadequate for the length of fence. Terminals were corroded, and the batteries were probably weak.

"I never seen a girl able to poke around electric stuff without blinkin' an eye. My pa says you and your ma and sister come from Portland. Don't know much about country life, I hear."

That didn't elicit a response from me. The trees and mountains and fresh air enchanted me. I couldn't quit thinking about Abigail who would never breathe the sweet, spicy scent of a Douglas fir again. Time to pump Jerry.

"We always lived in Portland. Don't know a thing about life in the country. You tell me, Jerry. What do you like best about living here—in the Compound, I mean."

His pause was significant, as though he might be sorting out things that he liked and I might find objectionable—such as statutory rape by forcing underage girls into marriages. "I like the fact that we are a special people with the sense to protect ourselves against the end of time. It's coming, Jenny. That's why we have our M-16s and enough food to last."

His unwavering, hypnotic, pale blue eyes fixed me in place; he was like a snake that can't blink. "I been to Spokane a few times with my pa. We men take the women over sometimes to sell their trinkets. Getting out for a spell seems to make them happy."

From Jerry's perspective, laboring over boiling oil to make soap, endlessly kneading dough to make bread, and bending over ancient sewing machines for hours to "sell their trinkets" to city women created a kind of happiness that the men enabled by letting them out of prison occasionally.

The brazen grin he flashed at me made my toes curl into the ends of my old tennis shoes. I would have stabbed him with the voltmeter but it made a puny sword.

"If you prove out, Jenny, I expect you'll be allowed to go, maybe next time. With my say-so."

Prove out? Give witness to something? Authenticate this jail? I turned away from Jerry so that he couldn't see the angry flush that I knew was spreading from my neck to the roots of my hair. "That would be a great kindness, Jerry. I wouldn't mind seeing a city again even though I'm becoming acclimated to this place." My wooden nose grew a foot. I gagged on bile of my own making.

I'd die to get to a city with a public telephone and a police station. I smiled wearily at Jerry, as though I was exhausted from pacing the fence and poking my voltmeter into the ground. That part had been easy. Jerry's liver. Jerry's spleen. Jerry's gall bladder. And, finally, Jerry's heart. I was charged enough to sprint right through a 10K. If I could get out of here on an "official" trip, I wouldn't have to break out of prison.

MY TOTE BAG felt heavier than usual when I hauled it upstairs to my room at the end of the day. Three books fell out of a small cloth-wrapped package: *A Commentary of the First Book of Euclid's Elements*, Dickens'

Bleak House and Jacqueline Susann's *Valley of the Dolls.* Eager to get away when Jerry brought me home, I had left my tote on the front porch for a couple of hours. Josh had kept his promise about the books. But the selections were odd.

We had discussed Euclid, but why would he select a book by Dickens about poor Esther, who might as well be motherless? And a book about "dolls," barbiturate use? If he was sending me a message, I wasn't getting it.

TINY FRIED BIRDS, picked clean of feathers and denuded of heads, feet, and wings made a spiritless pile on Maylene's best platter. As Mr. Darken chomped his way through bird bodies, Mother seemed particularly edgy, more animated than she'd been since we moved from the Retreat. She rolled her uneaten quail around her plate as though encouraging it to take flight.

"We read about Bathsheba today. Mrs. Barnes says if I study about poor, benighted women in the Bible, I'll better understand your religion." She looked toward the end of the table at Mr. Darken.

My ears perked up. For the first time in two weeks, she said "your religion," not "our religion." Looked as though Mother might be backsliding. Maylene and Marybeth seemed transfixed by the turn of the conversation.

"It appeared to me that King David was a window peeper of the first order. Just imagine, spying on a married woman who had gone all the way up to the top of a roof to bathe in privacy! Then, he got her pregnant and managed to have her husband killed."

"That's because . . ." the pause was lethal as Mr. Darken speared his fourth bird. "Because she stood on top of a building stark naked and tempted King David. Connived to get herself pregnant and her husband killed so that the wrath of God fell upon David. Just one of many temptresses starting with Eve."

As Mr. Darken deftly sliced breast meat away from both sides of a tiny wishbone, he dimmed my hopes for an easy exit from the Compound.

"You're right to bring up the subject of temptresses, Clara. Your girl here fits the bill. She's been causing some trouble at the Council level—between Elder Winner and Elder Bonner. Their boys have been good friends far too long to let something as silly as a girl come between them."

"You must be mistaken, Gomer. Jenny is a child without the slightest interest in boys—much less those two. Her father and I agreed long ago that she wouldn't be allowed to date until she's sixteen. That is a promise to him that I intend to keep." If Mother could shoot daggers from her eyes, I think GOD just got speared.

"I don't think your dead husband has much say-so in this neck of the woods. Pass me some more of that good gravy, Marybeth." A faint, greasy dribble on his chin attested to the success of Marybeth's quail gravy.

"First, she gallivants off into the canyon all day with Josh Barnes—who is *persona non gratia* around here at the moment. Then, she all but decks Enoch, who repays our family with these nice, plump quail. The boy has a forgiving spirit." The angry gleam in the eyes of Mr. Darken suggested that he didn't share that spirit.

"And now, after spending just one day with Jerry, she tried to convince him to ask his father to let her go to Spokane with him. It isn't going to happen, but she's managed to wrap that grieving young man around her little finger." As though a bolt struck him, he whirled around in his chair and pointed at Mother.

"Speaking of fingers, Clara. Where's the diamond ring? I said that you could wear it in the house for a while. Then, it needs to go back into the safe."

Maylene and Marybeth were sending throwing stars out of their eyes faster than Ninja warriors. It dawned on me—and probably Mother—that her two-carat diamond was a family heirloom and probably not finished with its conquests.

"It's somewhere in my room. I'll look for it later, Gomer." Mother responded almost too nonchalantly. "I want to show the girls what I made them. A surprise. Mrs. Barnes has been helping me learn how to make ceramic things that she bakes in her kiln."

A string of bright blue beads—like the donkey beads I've seen at flea markets—spilled out in front of Lorena. "You left brown places on them, Mother." Lorena was an exacting child. Very annoying at times.

"Your necklace is very special, Jenny. It's the first one I made." She placed a large lump of misshapen hard clay about the size of a quarter in front of me. She had painted an odd little flower on it and put a hole right through the center. She looped the leather thong around my neck and patted the medallion firmly against my chest. "It will bring you good luck. Something especially for you."

"Your skills at jewelry making are about on par with your bread making, Clara. Doesn't quite come off." Marybeth snorted. "Seems like you could learn to do something besides be ornamental."

"No one could make that charge against you, Marybeth." After being unjustly accused of "causing trouble," I was ready to take on the sisterwives or GOD himself.

Silence and the sucking of quail bones were the only sounds around the table, but there was a thick, pungent aura here, as though we'd all been cut loose from reality and were no longer part of the real world.

Mother said: "I'm taking Jenny up to her bedroom. I didn't raise my daughter to be rude to her elders."

Well. That was a nice retort. She put me in my place and took a sideswipe at Marybeth at the same time.

"It's about time you disciplined these girls, Clara. I won't have my family causing trouble in the community." With only Lorena left around the table, he pointed a stubby finger at her. "You take one bite of that quail, Lorena, before you turn up your nose at perfectly good food. Just one bite or I'll force it down your throat. I'm tired of your finicky ways."

Mother and I paused in the doorway. Lorena might be pigheaded about the food she would and wouldn't sample, but we had learned the hard way that when she declined food, it was best to leave her be.

"Here, you persnickety child. Just one little sliver with some nice gravy on it." Marybeth had joined Mr. Darken's platoon and was easing apart Lorena's clenched jaws. Maylene, wisely, had retreated to the far side of the room; Marybeth stood behind Mr. Darken and grinned maliciously.

Lorena gagged, flushed as purple as beet soup, thrust out her chest like a pouter pigeon and expelled the contents of her stomach with unerring accuracy on Mr. Darken and Marybeth.

Mother left Maylene to respond to the chorus of howls. Normally, not a demonstrative mother, she looped her arm over my shoulders and squeezed me against her as we walked up the stairs to the bedroom. After easing the door shut, her shoulders slumped and tears flushed her eyes.

"Don't pay any attention to Marybeth, Mother. She's just a jealous old hag. I like this thing you made. It's very . . . uh . . . natural." I held the crude, clay oval up and tried to determine whether the flower was a daisy or wilted lily.

"It's as ugly a thing as I could make."

I gave her an astonished look.

"It's valuable. There's a two-carat diamond ring cooked into that lump of clay. I doubt that anyone would try to take something that hideous away from you."

"But, that's your ring. Mr. Darken gave it to . . ."

"To Maylene and then to Marybeth and then to me and whoever comes next." She sank down on the bed next to me, sobbing quietly. "I've quit taking those pills that Gomer gives me every night so I can . . . relax." The way she said "relax" sounded as though it was a condition just this side of oblivion. "Valium. It softens the edges of the way things are."

"Diazepam, Mother. Only a doctor can prescribe them. They can be dangerous." At that moment, I remembered that Mr. Tomeh had asked me once if I could get him some "valley girls" to take with his Thunderbird. Suddenly, Josh's book selections began to make sense—just as my mother was making the kind of sense that frightened me.

"Something is going on between Mr. Darken and two of the elders. They were here last night late. I think that *something* involves you and one of their sons. A kind of deal. He's too cagey to let me know what he's up to. But, he's up to no good."

Mother put her hands on both sides of my face, gripping it as though she might be able to make me disappear. "If you get a chance, Jenny, and I don't know how you will, you have to get away. They watch everything we do. Mrs. Barnes tried to take Josh away after her husband was killed. They didn't make it to the county line. A deputy brought them back. These people pay off everyone."

I shuddered. So much for finding a phone to call the police.

Mother reached into her pocket and pulled out a wad of bills rolled with a rubber band. "Mr. Darken leaves his wallet lying around sometimes. I've turned into a thief as well as a fool. You might need this. I don't know where you can go, but the last I heard was that Hal, your uncle, had a fishing boat on the Oregon Coast."

I wanted to quiz her about this uncle of mine that she had mentioned twice—once at my father's graveside and now with tears streaming down her face. There wasn't time to retrieve lost relatives.

"Clara. Come to bed. I'm right put out with both your girls now. Some sympathy would be nice." The clarion call of Mr. Darken resounded up the stairs.

"Mother. I have a plan but don't want to say much right now. He might force you to . . ."

I rose and stared down at my weeping mother. Anything I told her could put my plans at risk. Maybe Valium acted like a truth serum, something they injected into the veins of spies to make them tell all.

I had been thinking about that fence and the great automatic sliding gate. If I could get the amperage high enough, it would flatten a herd of elephants. When Jerry punched in the key code, I moved like the quick-witted girl that I am over next to him and talked a mile a minute, watching as he punched in the code: 6666. Still set the same as when Mr. Darken used it. Whoever set the code had a bizarre sense of humor.

"You, Lorena and me. All of us need to go." I seemed to have moved into the parental role with Mother sobbing and me comforting her.

"Lorena's safe for now. These people don't marry off girls that young. When they start their periods, they're fair game. Men as old as Gomer have wives as young as you. Disgusting." Mother had stopped crying. "I do despise him. I'm a stupid, stupid woman. I was afraid of our poverty, afraid that you and Lorena wouldn't have a good life. So, I've brought you to this. Us, to this." Hopelessness took on a sense of desperation that I'd never heard my mother express, not even in our lowest moments after Daddy died.

"I need to playact with Gomer and try to act normal with my *sisterwives*. When I look dazed from the Valium, it keeps Gomer off guard—even though I've been flushing it for the past three days. Marybeth is stupid and vicious. I can't read Maylene. She acts friendly enough, but there's something behind her eyes. She barely tolerates Marybeth. I can't figure her out."

"Don't trust any of them, Mother. Not even Mrs. Barnes. She's a product of this place, this weird life. I thought Josh might be different. He may be on our side, but I don't trust anyone in this Compound."

Mother opened the door and turned to send me a final, tear-stained smile. I could hear her taking the steps slowly and fading away, like Eurydice heading back to Hades because Orpheus chose one more look.

CHAPTER 18

Two more days of checking fence with Adolph, as I fondly thought of him, caused me to speed up my fence project.

On day two, he came within a hair's breadth of touching my left nipple as he oh-so-casually reached across me to lower my window. New truck. They're automatic. On his side of the pickup.

With a bit of prodding, Adolph's conversation during the day escalated in tempo. Lots of negative comments about his friend Enoch. Lots of positive comments about where he fit in the hierarchy of eligible bachelors and how could I think otherwise—delivered with the subtlety of a club against the side of a cave woman's head.

Sometimes, I had the strangest sense that he forgot who I was and thought he was talking to Abigail—I had become his red-haired intended.

On day three, Adolph actually cupped my butt with both hands as he boosted me across a broken line of fencing. He stood preening on the other side of the fence, his thin thighs coming to a V in his crotch—like an upside-down fork in a tree stump with its knotty burl jutting out from his pants.

That took our relationship to a whole new level. There would be no day four.

Jerry Winner was coming on to me like the old bull that charged the electric fence to get at the heifers. The difference. I wasn't in heat. From the neck down, I was polar ice. I pulled out my little notebook and began coldly calculating electrical supplies for Mr. Darken to get at the farm supply store in Bonner's Ferry tomorrow.

I FAKED A bad case of flu the next morning by filching Mentholatum from Maylene's medicine chest to give me red eyes. The old-fashioned glass thermometer flashed up to 101 with a quick duck under warm water. A day in bed with *Valley of the Dolls* should prepare me for a clean, sober, drug-free life—and not detract from my sketches of how a voltage source drives a current around a circuit to deliver the maximum electrical energy into a resistor and back to the target, i.e., any CPRCer who dared to breach the jimmied gate.

That's how the day should have gone—and would have if someone hadn't let the horse out of the barn. I was on the lookout for Mr. Darken's truck with the supplies from Bonner's Ferry. So was that scarecrow Elder Grund with skin the color of lye soap that had just been dismissed from a Spokane hospital. From my upstairs window, I could see him poking around in the back of Mr. Darken's truck, frenziedly pointing at my supplies as though I were a foreign power importing material for a nuclear weapon.

I had primed Mr. Darken with selective information in case someone at the farm supply store was curious. "The wood posts and t-posts are generally OK, but you need better grounding and more powerful chargers all along the sections where you want to keep the wildlife out and livestock in." Wolves had gotten through to some early spring calves that very week, so Mr. Darken didn't take much convincing.

The erstwhile electrician, Elder Grund, whose heart seemed to be pumping like a body builder on steroids, wasn't convinced.

Mr. Darken dragged me out of my sick bed, red nose, high fever and all. I barely had time to hide Jacqueline Susann's masterpiece under the mattress. "Elder Grund says that no one would use this amount of stuff on a fence for animals. He says you're having us on. Or planning to electrocute half the county. He wants his voltmeter back."

Nervous over being caught in the act so to speak, I went back upstairs, grabbed the old voltmeter and stuck my knife into the black insulated cable, doing as much damage as possible, trying to make it appear that a rat had gotten to it.

Elder Grund flushed angrily, but I stood my ground. He might be the kingpin electrician for the Ward, but everything I'd seen—from fuse boxes to amateurish usage of cheap extension cords plugged together like procreating Japanese beetles—told me that he was an amateur at his trade. "Your equipment is crap. The fuse boxes in every building are worn out. It's a wonder this place hasn't gone up in flames." I thrust the voltmeter toward him. "Everyone uses digital voltmeters these days. You're living in the Dark Ages."

The arm lock that Mr. Darken put on me dropped me to my knees. "You do not talk to an Elder in that way. You apologize to him this instant!" Mr. Darken's thunderous voice amplified my pain.

The faintest smile twitched across a line of dentures that outpaced Mr. Darken's in terms of size and whiteness. Elder Grund's new stent—or whatever the doctors had used to recharge his heart—was working overtime. He was actually enjoying my suffering.

I was prepared to suffer more. "Little children are in the buildings you wired. You should be reported for endangering lives."

The fist that cracked against my head blissfully put me out of my misery. I woke briefly to the sound of my mother screaming at Mr. Darken, Marybeth screaming at my mother, and Mr. Darken shouting to someone on the phone. Then, I slept again. I think the flu invaded me because I'd lied about the virus earlier in the day.

WHEN I AWOKE the next morning, the house was as quiet as a tomb, as though I had been deserted. Aside from a black eye and a shoulder that was on the verge of dislocation, I felt tolerably well. The great electric fence caper had failed, but I knew a dozen weak spots where I could get through into the forest and halfway to Canada before anyone knew I was missing.

Lorena couldn't walk to Canada. Mother wouldn't. Not without both of her girls. I'd have to come up with another scheme. Savoring the thought of escape, I remembered my MacBook down in Mr. Darken's office. I could put an SOS on Facebook, Twitter, the FBI site and to the state governor, whoever that was.

After the chaos years ago at the Branch Davidians' compound in Texas, the FBI would be careful in storming the fort. No casualties would be allowed. But, trafficking in women and children was offensive to the civilized world. They'd eventually come.

They did. Mr. Darken, Elder Winner, Elder Bonner, and Elder Grund. They clomped into my bedroom like the Four Horsemen of the Apocalypse. When I opened my mouth to scream, Mr. Darken shoved pills into my mouth and held it closed until I was forced to swallow or die from lack of air. The pressure on my neck sent stars exploding like a poor man's Fourth of July into the cheap cellulose tiles of my bedroom ceiling. Then, the celebration ended.

I dreamed of red trucks and Hitler mustaches and goose-stepping soldiers; as brambles ripped my body, I crawled naked through a swamp of fetid water, dying of thirst. Then I reached a bubbling spring of the clearest, sweetest water I'd ever tasted and knew I was safe.

CHAPTER 19

It was just a dream, but the sun was streaming through a window covered with a pretty lace panel. A chilled bottle of water sat on a bedside table. I pushed back a down comforter and examined my body. All here. Still intact. The horsemen hadn't damaged the merchandise. However, I was buttoned up to my chin in someone's white cotton gown.

A rosy-cheeked woman with a soft, doughy body tiptoed across the room and looked down at me. "How do you feel, Jenny? I'm afraid that Mr. Darken might have overdone the tranquilizers. You've been asleep for almost twenty hours. We managed to get some water down you. You were very dehydrated."

She plumped up the comforter. "I'm Leah, Mr. Winner's third wife. I'll be taking care of you if that's all right. If you prefer to have Joanna, his second wife, she can sit with you a spell. We don't want you to be alone. Some girls have a bad reaction to tranquilizers."

"Where's my mother? My sister?" My voice was as raspy as sandpaper on rough wood.

"Your mother? Clara, I think she's called?" Leah looked at me for affirmation though I was sure she knew what my mother was called and was simply stalling, making meaningless conversation. The frozen glance I sent her didn't seem to perturb her.

"She's with her husband. He's looking after her. She had a little setback when the elders had to make some changes in living arrangements." The rosy cheeks had retreated into a malleable face that seemed to be waiting for something to register behind it.

I swung my legs to the floor and almost toppled out of the bed.

"You have to sit up carefully. You haven't had any-thing to eat. Those pills can make you wobbly." The killer grip of those plump little Pillsbury Doughboy hands settled me flat on my back.

A pillowy neck, the texture of old foam rubber, hung inches from my face. I wondered if vampires chose necks based on how attractive they were. This one would be safe. Grunting with pain, I shoved myself into an upright position.

"What do you mean about changes in living arrangements? My family lives in Mr. Darken's house—at least for now."

"Well, they did, but the elders have decided that you and Clara and Lorena aren't acclimating the way that Mr. Darken had hoped. So, for now, Mr. Darken and Clara will be together, like newlyweds." She giggled. "Working on the sacrament of marriage with the help of her sisterwives."

I froze at the bizarre image. "And Lorena?" I was almost afraid to ask.

"She's staying with the Johnsons, Abigail's family. I think you were a particular friend of that sad girl." There was something very coy about the way she rolled out "particular."

"The Johnsons have a girl about the same age as Lorena. Mr. Darken thinks it would be best for the child to spend quality time around a quiet little girl like Rebecca Johnson. He says having only adult company can warp a child."

He'd know about that, wouldn't he? He didn't have children around until he shanghaied Lorena, along with Mother and me. I relaxed and stretched my legs, hoping to dislodge Leah from the side of the bed. I had felt a kind of connection to Abigail's mother, as we had stood grieving over her casket. Lorena would be safer than she was with Mr. Darken or Marybeth with her arsenal of peach tree switches.

This time I moved my legs to the edge of the bed and sat up slowly. "Thank you, Leah, for looking after me. I certainly won't report you, but I've been kidnapped and that's a felony. Your so-called elders have really overstepped their bounds this time."

"No, dear. I don't think you understand. *You* crossed the bounds. The elders said that you were planning something having to do with the fence. They weren't sure if you intended to charge it or disable it—tinkering with our security." Leah's eyes popped wide, like trap doors with nothing much behind them, as though she struggled to remember her script.

"Women—and that includes girls—learn at a very young age that they are subservient to the will of their men through the priestly ordinances of our religion." Her eyes narrowed just a bit. "The men reward their women by looking out for them, being sure that they want for nothing."

Like enough sex? Equal division of property? Or first wife gets the lion's share? Elder Winner with his pork-pale skin and spindly legs didn't exactly look like a man who could provide everything that four healthy women, two of them half his age, could desire.

But I'd better control the mouth until the feet found the exit. "I'd like to have my clothes, now, Leah. I have things to do. I need to check on my mother and my sister. I want to be sure that Mrs. Johnson is willing to keep Lorena for now—and that my mother is OK with that decision."

"She doesn't have to be. She's in no state to make decisions about her children. She got quite hysterical when Mr. Darken reprimanded you for your disrespect to Elder Grund, the oldest member of our Council. That just isn't done, Jenny."

My tongue was unfurling faster than a flag in a high wind when I bit it. My big mouth got me here. My brain needed to get me out. I could wheedle with the best of them.

"I'd consider it a great kindness if I could have something to eat. A piece of dry toast would be fine." I sent out a weak smile.

"Oh no. I'll bring you a very good breakfast. Jeremiah, my stepson—I think of the boy as my own—wouldn't be happy if we didn't treat you with the utmost hospitality. He had words with his pa last night. Didn't like the fact that Elder Bonner and Mr. Darken were carrying you in what he called a 'familiar' manner. You were dead weight in that skimpy attire covered with cats and hello. I got rid of the silly things."

I flashed another weak smile. Hello Kitty hadn't made it past Leah. And, it was clear to me that Adolph didn't want anyone else handling the merchandise. He let that slip a couple of times when we were checking the fence. Something about "promised girls" being bound. I had conjured up an image of Chinese women wobbling along on four-inch feet. It's a good thing the CPRC men needed an active workforce of women.

When Jerry was nattering on about his expectations for desirable females as we walked the fence, he had called me Abby twice and didn't seem to realize his mistake. Josh had told me that Jerry Winner had a screw loose. Now, I was a guest in the house of that Neo-Nazi, being tended by a sisterwife without a tight screw in her head.

"Stay put, Jenny. I'll hustle down to get your breakfast and a wet rag for your face. Breakfast in bed. A real treat." As Leah backed out of the room, I heard the distinct click of an outside bolt.

My current confinement was not what I'd call a treat with Elder Winner's sisterwives guarding the fort. I was imprisoned in an attic bedroom that actually had an old-fashioned slop jar under the bed.

From the window, it was a sheer drop three stories down to the ground. Not a tree limb or a foothold in sight. The view might be considered splendid if one liked peering into the back doors of a dozen houses across a small creek. I gasped at my good fortune.

The morning sun flashed a thousand diamonds off the panes of a greenhouse. Not more than 100 yards beyond the creek was Josh's house. Or, it was his house before the elders hustled him into SYM confinement. If I could find a mirror, I could flash Morse code messages. If I only knew the code. I knew SOS; that would have to do. The elders had left my tote bag with the knife and coil of paracord behind.

Until I could figure out how to get a message to Josh—not that he'd pay any attention to it—a well-thumbed Bible and a 1955 Sears Catalogue were my entertainment. Along with visits by Elder Winner's sisterwives. They were uniformly aghast that I had no skills for surviving the apocalypse. I couldn't milk a cow, candle an egg, sew a straight line, or slice up a tough old cow for jerky.

After two hours with them, I turned to religion. When I got tired of Bathsheba's acquiescence to that bully of a king, I studied the different kinds of girdles available to women in 1955. Whalebone corsets had disappeared, but elastic straps of every size and shape girded up the female population. I imagined Jerry Winner trying to feel me up through one of those barriers.

Just when the image was sending me into projectile vomiting, a key turned in the lock and the man himself shot a coy grin at me. "They treatin' you OK, Jenny? Was the breakfast Leah brought you OK? Need anything?"

"Freedom, Jerry. A telephone so I can report a violent crime. My own clothes. And, my mother. I want to see my mother."

The cackle of laughter might have shaken me had I not seen little polar caps forming behind those pale blue eyes. I was terrified.

Adolph's purposefully comforting words were even more horrifying. "The elders and Mr. Darken shouldn't have frightened you like that. If I'd been there, I wouldn't have allowed them to carry you. I could lift up a little thing like you without even breathing hard."

Meaning. He approved of the action, just not the method. Jerry stood in the open door, shifting his weight from one foot to the other. "The door has to stay open, but I can visit with you as much as you like. Beings how things are just about settled. Would be settled if Enoch could keep his trap shut."

I suddenly knew exactly how Persephone felt after she had eaten pomegranate seeds in the nether region. Leah's pancakes might have condemned me to life in Hades with the god-king of the underworld. The wheedling, coaxing, be-on-her-best-behavior Jenny Hatchet needed to sing like a Siren.

"Those pills Mr. Darken pushed down my throat make me feel really bad, Jerry." I modestly cast a pitiful look at him as I pulled the cotton gown tight across my braless chest. "I really need fresh air. You could take me for a walk outside. That would be nice of you."

He walked over to the small window overlooking Mrs. Barnes's greenhouse, shook it loose from ancient calking, and sent it flying upward. "There. Fresh air."

As though resisting the temptation of what lay beneath that coarse cotton gown, he stepped back, bent over and placed his big calloused palms on both sides of my face. "Until things is resolved with my mourning state, no way can I break the rules, Jenny. You might sweet talk one of Pa's wives into taking you as far as the back garden. But, I doubt it. We tend to follow orders around here."

With a curt little salute, like Hitler acknowledging the fallen French at the Arc de Triumph, Jerry Winner backed out of the room and firmly slid the bolt in place.

From the open window, about a hundred yards away, I could see Lorena playing with other children in a field, her saggy skirt luffing like a spinnaker as she dashed from one side of the play area to the other. For some reason, I thought of Wordsworth seeing "the children sport upon the shore." And his gloomy reminder that the "shades of the prison-house begin to close."

Being locked up in a stark attic room with nothing but the Bible and an ancient catalog gave me too much time to think. As I watched those children playing outside in a world so replete with the marvels of nature, anger overwhelmed me. No one has the right to interrupt that process of discovery that is the right of all children—by defining their futures.

I recalled that year after my father's death with bittersweet memories. Something had been broken. The jigsaw puzzle that our lives became didn't quite fit, but we had all but one of the pieces. Mother, Lorena and I had each other; given time, we could have salvaged our life—until a serpent snaked his way into Portland and took us to his Eden.

We never could put anything together here. A crazed man with missing golden tablets and a council of old men who thought they were direct descendants from King David made the rules without much regard to the seven deadly sins. Added to the list were a few of their own making: ignorance, slavery, and destruction of dreams.

CHAPTER 20

Without anything but the morning sun and then a gibbous moon to divert me, I slept dreamlessly hour after hour. Like the three monstrous Gorgons on guard, the Winner sisterwives carried in trays of food as I watched to see if scales were forming and beards growing on the women. After eating, I felt spaced out, stupefied, as though I couldn't run if someone left the door unbolted.

On what I thought must be my second day of imprisonment, Leah brought me a stack of clothes. "These belonged to my oldest girl. Married now to one of the Tefetellers in the ward over by Boise City," she said triumphantly as though I should know where the Tefetellers fit in the scheme of the Chain of Being. Leah didn't look old enough to have a married daughter, but I didn't dare comment. "You can have a bath downstairs."

The enclosed wooden staircase spiraled precipitously down. I clung to Leah's arm, grateful not to feel any scales. "Elder Winner and Jerry are downstairs," she confided. The Gorgons had put their men on guard. "You can set for a meal with us if you like."

I didn't. A wave of nausea swept over me as I sunk down on the bottom step. Steaming water rose in clouds of fog from a huge, claw-footed bathtub. "Shampoo's on the table by the tub in the green bottle. I make it myself. Baking soda and water. You can have a bit of privacy, Jenny, but you are not to lock this door. I'll be just outside."

I turned on the tap again so that Leah couldn't hear me rummaging through the medicine cabinet. Nothing of use. Not so much as a rusty razor blade.

Immersing myself in warm water with a bar of lye soap that I had probably cooked brought me out of my zombie daze. The baking soda shampoo was surprisingly refreshing. The clothes of Leah's daughter sagged around me, but I was too exhausted to care. The simple act of bathing had worn me out. Something was very wrong here.

The something that was wrong had turned me into Rita Henchly, the zonked out girl in my freshman class in Portland, whose eyes went from being big as saucers to half-closed, opaque, glittering slits. The "Barb Queen" some of the kids called her when they weren't trying to buy Ludes or Sopors from her. The counselor who cleaned out Rita's locker refused to tell anyone where Rita had gone. It probably didn't matter; Rita wanted to be somewhere else.

Someone had clobbered me with Quaaludes or a drug as potent. From now on, I'd avoid drinking the cocoa that Leah brought up every night.

THE NEXT DAY, Leah surprised me with a grudging announcement: "You have a visitor. Maylene, your other mother." I didn't think of Maylene as a mother. I tried not to think of Maylene at all. As the first wife in the Darken household, she should have held the place of honor and power, but next to that hard charger Marybeth, she was almost invisible.

Maylene struggled through the narrow door to my bedroom carrying a green spidery plant the size of a bushel basket. Leah trailed behind her, holding up the end of an intricate macramé plant hanger. "Mrs. Barnes sent you this from her greenhouse. She said you were particularly fond of aspidistras. They need to be hung. I think that old hook above the window will work fine, Leah."

The two of them struggled to get the plant settled into its macramé cradle and looped over the curtain rod but gave up, putting it on a stool in the corner of the room. They stood back to admire their work.

"Mrs. Barnes sprinkled those little clay balls with fertilizer on top of the soil. She says you just push one down to the roots every week or so. She said you know what aspidistras like, Jenny."

The only thing I knew about aspidistras was that Dorothy Sayers used one to kill off a cheeseparing character in *Busman's Holiday*. I had never had a conversation with Mrs. Barnes about anything. Something was afoot here, and it was best to play along.

Maylene took the first step. "I'd like to visit with my stepdaughter alone, if you don't mind, Leah," Maylene said dismissively.

"Stepmothers-in-law carry about the same weight as stepmothers, Maylene. Beings you're a guest, I wouldn't deny you a few minutes alone." Leah waddled out the door, looking missish.

All that nattering on about stepdaughters and step-mothers-in-law made me nervous. The great, spindly aspidistra was giving me Botanophobia.

"Lie back down, Jenny. You look ill and thin. What are these people feeding you?"

"Yellow Jackets, Red Devils. Who knows?" The blank expression on Maylene's face told me that she hadn't a clue. "Something similar to what Mr. Darken gives Mother to take off the edge." Maylene nodded.

"Marybeth's idea. When Gomer called from Portland to say he'd found a new sisterwife for us with two beautiful children, Marybeth practically came unhinged. She said there had been no hint that Gomer was dissatisfied even though neither of us has borne him a child. I think she got the calming pills from Leah." Maylene reached down and laid her hand softly alongside my face. It was the first time that she had ever touched me.

"Gomer was out of line in bringing non-members to the Compound. The way you sassed him gave me heart-burn. As an only son, Gomer was raised with a sense of entitlement. He doesn't cotton to different opinions," she said through pursed lips.

"Your mother just seemed so lost, as though she had mislaid her own life." Maylene paused as though trying to sort out some connection between "calming pills" and Mother's abyss. She brightened. "Lorena is just the delight of my life. I've never been around young children much. That child really likes me. I could tell." Her face fell.

"Marybeth couldn't abide seeing that kind of affection. She started in on her schemes the minute that Gomer called to let us know he was bringing a new family to join us. Whipping that child because she wanted her kitten inside was the last straw." A woebegone expression settled on Maylene's face.

"Maylene, it's about time for Jenny's evening meal." Leah's voice shrieked up the stairs.

"They don't want me here. They don't want anyone but Winners around you, Jenny. Enoch Bonner is making foolhardy statements against Jerry. That's causing some trouble with the Council." Maylene moved over to the window and stared fixedly for a moment at something outside. "I only get to see Lorena when Mrs. Johnson allows me to visit her. Selfish like. As though she might replace Abigail."

She turned abruptly, her face readjusted to show nothing. "The women here learn submission from childhood. Control is what we show. Emotions bring us low."

Doggerel from Maylene was more than I could bear while flat on my back wearing the fat clothes of Leah's oldest daughter. Allowing us solitude was more than Leah could bear. We could hear her walloping the stairs as she brought up my evening tray.

"You don't eat with the family?" Maylene gaped at me.

"Don't want to. Want out of here." My speech sounded slurred even when I was trying to spell out precisely what I wanted.

Just as Leah turned the key in the lock, Maylene clasped me to her as though she might have been the shipwrecked sailor and I the port. It made me uncomfortable. The words she hissed in my ear didn't. "Mrs. Barnes is a very purposeful woman. On your side, just as I am. I'm watching out for Clara. You need to watch out for yourself."

With that, she left, brushing Leah aside as she might an annoying insect.

"She outstayed her welcome. You're not up to having company. I told Jerry that we should keep you in the family's bosom until things is settled." She waved a printed leaflet in my face. "*Women's Wisdom*. It's a little pamphlet our group at church puts out. Just some thoughts and scripture to cheer us up. Sometimes a good recipe. Maylene used to put in some of her nice poetry, but I guess she hasn't had time since your family moved in." Leah looked perplexed. "She should have more time now."

She went back to the door. "I almost forgot. Maylene brought over your old tennis shoes and jacket." She tossed Bob Marley into a heap on the floor and dumped my tennis shoes on top. "I hope you'll refrain from wearing them in this house."

She plumped up my pillow, went over to inspect the aspidistra, and smacked her lips with displeasure. "That big old thing will be a bother to keep watered. I can get it out of here for you."

"Leave it, Leah. Green plants cleanse the air." I think I had heard that somewhere; these people were fixated on cleaning, so she might keep her predatory hands off my aspidistra so I could try to turn it into some kind of weapon—the way that Dorothy Sayers' villain did. "What is this?" I pointed to an oversized steaming crockery pot.

"Extra hot chocolate to help you sleep better. Jerry said you were looking a bit peaked and were right testy when he stopped by for a visit early this morning."

Yes, I was testy. Petulant and crabby as a bear prodded out of hibernation. Adolph had ventured into my den while I was still asleep and groped me under the down comforter. His slimy fingers circled first one breast and had started on the other when I awoke. A hand with dirty fingernails clamped onto my mouth.

"Shush, Abby. You'll wake the house. I was just adjusting your covers to keep you warm."

I didn't know if the egg on his face was from an obvious lie or whether he had just realized he'd called me by name of his dead intended. He had sheepishly backed out of the room before I could unfurl my ballistic tongue. I got as far as "lecher," "defiler," and stopped midway through "ravisher." That word made Jerry appear too dashing. Dirty fingernails and pussyfooting into my bedroom while I was asleep did not add up to the princely rescuer of Rapunzel.

Something else did. I waited until I could hear the last clomp of Leah's shoes on the staircase and bolted out of bed. I staggered, woozy, probably from last night's chocolate and lack of exercise. I lifted a piece of the macramé hanger. It wasn't hemp. It was paracord, yards and yards of it, twisted and knotted into intricate shapes to form a cradle for the potted plant; additional thick strands made a long hanger.

The knots were tight with no space between the weavings, dense with lengths of paracord, like dozens and dozens of survival bracelets that could be unwound for emergency situations.

I picked at it until my fingers almost bled. Maylene had said something about pushing fertilizer into the roots of the plant. I dug around little clay lumps until I touched plastic. A Victorinox Swiss Army knife popped into my hand with several wicked little tools packed inside that lovely red shell.

Both blades would work nicely on Jerry's carotid. I didn't think that's what Mrs. Barnes had in mind. The knife's hook and screwdrivers would make short work of unraveling the knots. Almost forty feet with two hundred pounds of tensile strength should get me down two stories. I could drop the rest of the way.

CHAPTER 21

For a place full of boisterous children and quarrelsome sisterwives, the house was eerily silent at nightfall. Noiseless watchers might be by every window and door. I had turned off my lamp and pulled apart tightly woven cord in the dark for the past hour. Before the boys from SYM headed toward the dairy barn at five o'clock the next morning, I needed to be deep into the forest. I shivered at the thought. My hoodie, tennis shoes, and a hand-me-down skirt and blouse were the only defense against a cold night in the woods.

I knew the gate code, but didn't dare use a guarded exit. If I could stay just this side of the main compound fence and out of the line of spotlights, I would probably find the tracks that Josh and I had followed into the canyon. I knew where the weak spots were in the fence down there. Elder Grund might have recharged that section. The pulse duration would probably be under 3/1000's of a second and not even sting me if I touched a wire.

Leah's platter of beef brisket lay congealed in fat. Grabbing the catalog, I yanked out pages of headless women in girdles, wrapped up slices of meat, and stuffed them into my pocket. Slathering the big hunk of bread with butter, I pushed it into the other pocket. I ate the bowl of mashed potatoes and gravy and avoided the jug of chocolate as though it seethed with Black Death bacteria.

The moon arched toward the west. I bent out from the window, trying to gauge the distance. Odd, almost inhuman, sounds troubled the early spring night. I tested the paracord. It was so thin that sliding down, hand over hand, would be torturous.

The sturdy brogues that Leah had loaned me thrust their fat, wide leather tongues out temptingly. I sliced them off, almost relishing the agony that Leah would experience. Cupped into my hands, they would make perfect protectors for sliding. I cut two small lengths off my cord and sliced Leah's down comforter across the middle, rolling half of it into a tight scroll. Goose feathers floated around like an unseasonal snowstorm; the comforter would be as warm as a down sleeping bag.

Food and knife in pockets. Hoodie zipped. Tennis shoes with no socks. I was ready except for one very basic need—my family. Escaping from the Compound without Mother and Lorena was a serious act of betrayal. From the moment we drove through those locked gates into this perverted world, I had begun planning our escape together.

When my plan to recreate Old Sparky, the electric chair in Sing Sing, failed with Elder Grund's untimely arrival, I should have kept my mouth shut, pleaded ignorance, and figured out another plan. I guess the thought of sending 2,450 volts through one of the elders or Jerry Winner struck me as justice. My battery-powered contraptions wouldn't have packed such a wallop—just enough juice to frighten the natives away from the gate until we could make our getaway in Mr. Darken's Chrysler.

The only getaway in store for me was to some kind of wacky sealing ceremony. If I had to spend eternity with Jerry, I'd opt for a seat on Old Sparky. A strong breeze scented with pine and fir fluttered the lace panel on the window. Tears sprang to my eyes. The flora and fauna here made this part of Idaho a kind of Eden, what it must have been like before Adam tried to take control by naming every living creature.

I moved the iron bedstead inch by inch over against the wall with the window, tied one end of the cord to it, dropped my bedroll out the window, and slithered backwards over the sill and into space.

One leather shoe tongue lasted for about five seconds as I tried to coil part of the cord around my waist and rappel down the side of the house without making any noise. Controlling my impact against the house took all my strength. When I was midway down the second story, alongside the main bedroom wing, a light flashed on.

I froze, hanging in full view in front of a bedroom window. A shadow moved across the room, opened a door and disappeared down the hall. I clutched the paracord to swing myself sideways, away from the window, when the second shoe tongue twisted out of my grip.

My 110 pounds testing the strength of nylon paracord was no problem. Feeling something warm and sticky in my palms and realizing that it was my own blood was serious. About fifteen feet above prickly stubs of the sisterwives' rose garden, the pain shooting through my hands overwhelmed my fear of heights. I dropped. The sound vibrations must have rattled the lightning rods on the roof.

Lying like one of those sausage-shaped sea cucumbers that sprawl on sandy ocean bottoms, I undulated slightly to determine if anything was broken. The light from the second story went out. Nothing stirred. I felt as though every living thing in the field beyond me held its breath to see if I could actually rise, stretch, collect my bedroll and run the best 10K I'd ever managed.

I did. The dodgiest path I'd ever mastered stretched out before me with bright spotlights highlighting the gates and strands of electric wire inches away from me as I headed along the fence line toward what I thought was the canyon.

The path up toward the edge of the canyon seemed to be no more than a trail as the lights from the front of the Compound dimmed behind me. A coyote or a wolf sent up a lone howl, raising the hairs on my neck.

The moon dropped behind a huge cluster of firs then sent the palest sliver of light flashing off the fence. If I stayed exactly on the path, I should be traveling parallel to the fence.

When I was having a picnic with Josh and checking out his abs under his t-shirt, I should have been paying more attention to the fence. I did remember a weak point where the fence sagged above the boggy creek bed. A fir tree branch straddled the fence just ahead of me.

Water and electrical currents are bad combos. Sort of like oversized fries and drinks. Both can be lethal, but this one can stop you in your tracks. The ground was gummy. My tennis shoes were floundering in thick mud. I dropped to my hands and knees, pushed my bedroll ahead of me, then flattened military style to wiggle under the wires dangling above.

"Free at last! Thank God Almighty, we are free at last!" I whispered the words of Martin Luther King, Jr.; as I lay facedown on the spongy ground, I made a vow to always celebrate his holiday.

By the time I followed the trail up the other side of the canyon and entered the forest, I no longer had any sense of direction. I might be heading straight back to the Compound or to a public road where they could be patrolling. They might have alerted the local sheriff by now and plastered a wanted poster on every storefront.

For now, I'd stick to the forest. The path splayed into an old logging road that seemed to stretch on forever. Bears, wolves and cougars might attack me, but, for now, I wanted to be far away from humans until I found one I could trust.

Whomp! I fell across something as big as a millstone, plunging headlong into a nearby mound of soft dirt. A stabbing pain shot up my shin. The waning moon's wavering beams lit the clearing around me where tombstones marched at an angle, like exhausted soldiers coming home from battle.

My friend Abigail had been tucked in next to her grandfather, a "fine, monogamous man" her mother had advised me as we watched Abigail's casket being lowered into eternity. I had just tripped over the slab covering his grave and landed face down on Abigail's new grave.

Without moving any of my limbs, I began sobbing, crying in that self-absorbed way that children weep when they know that no one can comfort them. Escaping was behind me. Now, I had to mourn what I'd left behind. Or, maybe I was just crying for Abigail.

She was a girl who couldn't even feel nostalgia for her lost adolescence. Matched up by her parents and Elder Winner, she seemed reconciled to her "intended" Jerry. Yet, I could remember how her eyes sparkled when she pointed out her friend Zeb. All that Abigail could imagine was a narrow path that led from childhood to a marriage bed—with only a vague notion that something in her world was broken.

I pushed myself up, started to smooth over the still-rough soil on her grave, and stopped. Abigail's mother often visited her grave. A cluster of early daffodils stood at the end where a stone would sometime rest: "as soon as her father lets loose of the money," her mother told me, the bitterness in her eyes more meaningful than she would admit.

If she saw my handprints on the damp soil, she might guess I had been there to say my goodbye again to Abigail. She might let Mother know I had made it this far. I felt confident that she wouldn't tell anyone. I made two new handprints up by the vase of wilted daffodils and took off in a direction that I hoped was south. I didn't want to end up in Canada. The border officials would probably ship me back to the Compound.

BY MY INTERNAL clock, I guessed that I had been traveling fast for about two hours, too exhausted to keep up my current pace. Considering that I must have jumped ship about two or three o'clock, daybreak was still a couple of hours away. I needed to sleep and eat. I pulled out the cold slices of brisket, lined them up on the buttered bread and munched away.

The thick mats of needles beneath towering fir appeared to be well traveled by something. Probably elk or deer. Or bears. I could barely make out a thicket of something in a small clearing and moved over closer. It might be parsnip flower buckwheat. The thick, woody stems should have clusters of small yellow blooms.

The shin I cracked against Grandfather Johnson's tomb oozed, but it was too dark to access the damage. Couldn't be too serious if my tibia had been pumping along for two hours. Untying Leah's down comforter, a little the worse for wear, I wrapped it around my shoulders, wriggled into a low-lying mass of shrubs, and fell into an exhausted sleep.

CHAPTER 22

A piercing "sheck-sheck-sheck" jolted me awake. The morning sun filtering weakly through the dense firs sparked a Steller Jay into an indigo fire. He sat on a branch just over my head, fussing like a colicky baby. I was in his space. It was beautiful space with lush firs and pines. Just beyond, the ground swelled into a kind of ridge.

With a tongue salt-swollen from Leah's brisket, I needed water to keep going. I rolled my ragged comforter into a tight tube and tied the ends. Just over the swell, I could see sticky geraniums that were just opening pinkish blossoms. I recalled that Josh pointed them out as we were heading down the canyon toward the creek. He said they like moist soil. Water must be nearby.

Deer tracks were everywhere along the muddy bank. A stream wound just along the edge of the ridge and disappeared under an outcropping of rock. Greenish algae floated on most of the water. Small pockets of brownish, scummy water settled into animal tracks. I wasn't that desperate.

Just at the point where the stream seemed to be ending, small puddles of clear water had collected on a slab of limestone. I bent over and sipped cautiously. Untreated water in the wild could be dangerous. Untreated thirst could be fatal. I slurped up water faster than the Andrea Doria.

With the sun on my left, I angled a bit southwest and headed down an old logging or mining road. I knew that mine waste and tailings had polluted the Coeur d'Alene Lake and River. Our social studies teacher in the eighth grade had shown us photos of what a hundred years of uncontrolled mining could do to the environment.

As a project we all wrote letters to the US Forest Service and Fish and Game Departments to encourage the Superfund cleanup. The road I was trotting along probably led to an old mine. It was so overgrown; the only traffic I might meet would be an elk or deer.

Or Delhi Belly and Montezuma's Revenge hitching a ride with me. I doubled up with a stabbing pain that could be anything from an appendicitis attack or an epidemic of raging bacteria. Vomiting and diarrhea struck at the same time with the same intensity. The primeval forest rang with the sounds of retching and my struggle to find leaves or moss or anything to substitute as toilet paper. Desperately, I tore off strips of Leah's down comforter.

My violent innards erupted from both ends for at least another hour. Disgusting, perspiring and weak, I curled up along the side of a faint trail on a mat of fir needles; past feeling fear, I almost hoped that a wild animal would haul me away. Then I went out like a light.

THE STRANGEST DREAM I've ever had surrounded me with heaves and grunts and carried me like a baby through a forest. A face that might or might not wear Josh's dimples popped in and out of view like a puppet behind a dark curtain, as though the holder of the strings was teasing me.

A cart or a wagon or something with wheels moved so quickly that I could hardly feel the rasp of a dog's tongue on my face. Or, it could have been a mountain lion playing with its food. The cat family likes to play with dinner.

Coldplay's "Fix You" blasted into my dream. "When you try your best but you don't succeed . . . when you feel so tired but you can't sleep." In my dream I wept a waterfall of tears.

My mother, wearing that frilly yellow dress that my father loved, watched me coldly from the pew of a church where a dozen Maylenes sat on one side of her and a dozen Marybeths on the other.

Her face flushed with crying, Lorena bopped down the aisle flinging the blossoms of stinging nettles left and right.

Along the front of the altar, a line of elders, wearing the black robes of the Volturi, flashed big, square, blood-dripping dentures. I thought I might have been the bride, but I could no longer feel my legs moving or my arms forming a cross to fend off vampires. The voices around me were harsh and then soft before they faded into nothing at all.

THE BLANKET ON top of me was a brightly striped Hudson Bay and warm past imagining. The face bending over me belonged on one of those hot GQ male models, sculpted like a Greek statue and airbrushed into every girl's fantasy.

"You finally waking up?" The voice had that smoky quality of Nat King Cole, the kind of voice that goes right up your backbone and settles into your heart.

"Let her rest, Heath. She's a sick girl." A woman with skin the shade of warm mocha coffee and threads of gray lining the center part of her sleeked down hair replaced the GQ model that moved just to the left of my line of sight.

Behind him, a gleaming pine log wall soared at least twenty feet before splaying out into thick beams that crisscrossed the ceiling above me. Next to me, an open fire smelling of piñon popped with bright sparks. Muted woven rugs covered a flagstone floor. I was not back in the Compound. Jerry Winner was not waiting for me behind the vanguard of Volturi. I might be in Paradise, but I was too afraid to inquire.

The seraph, highest in the order of angels, moved to my bedside and beamed from ear to ear as a canticle came out of his mouth: "You're safe. You're on the Rez."

End of Book One of the Land Trilogy

Coming Soon! Land of the Bong Tree is the second novel in the Land Trilogy featuring Jenny Hatchet.

LAND OF THE BONG TREE

When fifteen-year-old Jenny Hatchet escapes from a forced "Celestial Marriage" in the *Land of Nod*, she finds temporary refuge on a reservation with the eccentric and charming Earnshaw family.

Stricken with guilt for leaving her mother and little sister in a polygamy compound, Jenny faces new emotional problems. She's attracted to both Healthcliff Earnshaw and her rescuer Josh Barnes—life-long best friends.

As Jenny searches for a long-lost uncle who might help her rescue her mother and sister, death strikes on the reservation.

Land of the Bong Tree leads Jenny to a new understanding of the value of family and friends, but her independent nature sets her on a dangerous path in this second novel of the Land Trilogy.

Another novel by Peggy Gardner

A WINDING SHEET

The dark and twisted past of her ancestor, Octavius Wolfe, ensnares his only living descendant in a web of century-old murders as Isabella Wolfe, a young physician, returns to her ancestral home in Southern Oklahoma.

A Winding Sheet entangles Isabella in a past that will not be denied in spite of her self-imposed exile for fifteen years. Desperate to discover the link between recent deaths and the hundred-year-old bones of two young girls in her family cemetery, Isabella challenges an instrument of death that hangs by her own family tree.

A Winding Sheet takes Isabella into a sinister world where her great-great grandfather's dream of an empire threatens the life of his only living descendant.

Available now at Amazon.com

What reviewers are saying about *A Winding Sheet:*

"I was hoping the story would never end, because it was so beautifully written, just like a song that you could listen to over and over again."

—E. F.

"A thoroughly enjoyable, superbly crafted book. An enthralling novel with an authentic sense of the stark atmosphere of Southern Oklahoma."

—G. H.

Gardner's lush, evocative descriptions of the Oklahoma landscape are those of a writer lovingly familiar with her subject, her keen medical insight that of an observant insider. This masterfully crafted and detailed novel will have you on the edge of your seat."

—J. M.

ACKNOWLEDGMENTS

Many thanks to my friends and relatives who have read *Land of Nod* and suggested improvements, especially the Bandon Writers Group.

I am indebted to Debbie O'Byrne for her brilliant cover designs.

ABOUT THE AUTHOR

Peggy Gardner began her career as a journalist, taught English Literature, managed medical education, clinics and research for a major hospital, and has traveled extensively with her husband, daughter, and son. She currently resides in Oregon for the incomparable splendor of its coast.

Made in the USA
San Bernardino, CA
16 May 2016